Raid In Lincoln County

James Hollmann

DEDICATION

Posthumously to Marvin Long, a gentleman, horseman and friend.

Also to those who came before us, everyone from every race who lived in the American Frontier West period of our country's history. Those brave souls chose to live a colorful life others could only dream of and gave us the rich history we enjoy. Without their strength we wouldn't be here today. Since that period of history is over, the rest of us have no options. We can only dream of such a life.

James Hollmann

CONTENTS

ACKNOWLEDGMENTS

I thank God (and my parents) for life itself, and for the influence you've had on me.

I'd like to thank Marvin Long, who taught me about horses. Whenever I have an equine problem I temper my response with memories of him and things usually work out fine. Mr. Long and his daughter, Amy Kutrufis, are responsible for giving me the first push toward writing. Thank you both.

Thank you also to my dear friends Jose, Philo and Tim. All of you taught me your ways and trust me with your way of life. You accept me as one of "you" and have my utmost respect.

To Johnny and my shooting family, you are truly wonderful people.

To our military and police veterans to include my son, Tim, thank you for your service to our country.

Last but not least I must thank my family, especially Kathy. You know why.

CHAPTER ONE

When the hail stopped I mounted up and headed north toward Lincoln. I was hoping to cover as much ground as I could before the rain stopped, for it would erase my tracks up to that point. Just a few hours before I had been enjoying a peaceful ride while at the same time scouting a place to wait out the storm I could see headed my way.

The dark clouds were getting nearer and just as I crossed the ridge into Crooked Canyon the wind picked up and the temperature dropped suddenly. It looked like there was a vertical bluff in the next draw that might offer shelter from the wind and rain so I loped my gelding in that direction. The underside of that bluff was a good spot alright, but it was occupied. I was hoping they wouldn't mind some company 'till the storm passed. Coming in from the direction I did, I was right up on them before I realized what they were up to. There were two cowhands branding horses and had about a dozen head of good stock tied to some scrub oaks. Some wore the "long rail" brand (a straight line from hip to shoulder) which is John Chisum's mark. Including the Morgan they just finished, a few wore fresh "arrow" brands. James Dolan from Lincoln had a ranch down on the Pecos and used that brand (an arrow from hip to shoulder).

They must of figured me for a Chisum rider and just opened up on me with their pistols right off. If I turned for cover I figured to catch some lead and the horse they had a hold of distracted them some so I spurred my horse into a run right at 'em, firing my own colt as I went. My first shot went wide and burned the horse one of them was holding. The horse reared and knocked the first man down. I put a hole near the Bull Durham tag hanging from the other man's shirt pocket, and ran my horse over the first man as he struggled to get to his feet. After about 75 yards I slowed my gelding to a stop and turned to look back. The man I'd run down was getting slowly to his feet but the other man never would. What worried me were the three or four riders I could see off in the distance. They were riding toward this camp, and if they were in cahoots with these two I'd be in trouble. I reloaded my pistol before heading west, up the canyon. With any luck I'd cross the Rio Felix as the rain started. This far up, the canyon should fill pretty quickly with rainwater and might slow down anyone following me.

Well I made it across the Felix in the rain alright, but when I crossed the ridge into Monument Canyon the hail started falling. Here in the high desert hail could get big enough to kill a man or horse if it hits just right, and I had no intention of getting caught in it for long. I holed up under a rocky ledge that with the wind as it was, sheltered a large enough area for both my horse and I. That was almost an hour ago, and now that the hail stopped I was again headed for Lincoln. Since I probably had riders hunting me I'd keep clear of the more open country and head west toward the mountains that were homelands of the Mescalero Apache. If I could make it into the pinion and juniper country of the foothills I figured to head north. The trees would give me some cover, and I surely would like to build a fire tonight after the soaking that storm had given me. I picked my way along, keeping to the rocky canyon bottom, near the water's edge. It was chancy, since I could expect more water to swell the runoff stream at any time. But I needed to stay concealed on low ground for the time being. It was my thinking that once the water did rise it would cover any signs of my passing with dirt, rocks, and other debris. If I chose a safer and more visible path, it would only remain safe for a short time, since I would leave sign my pursuers would find easy to follow. Riding careful like that I managed to make it across Twin Buttes Canyon and finally made camp in the trees near Deadman Lake. There were two large boulders that years ago had broken off the top of a thirty foot drop, and they made a snug place to bank a fire and warm up during the night. There was a small grassy area nearby that was partially sheltered by the small cliff. That is where my strong black gelding rested and fed through the night. I knew the men on my trail would find it difficult, if not impossible to find my trail at first. But if they persisted long enough they might get lucky and find some small sign that could give them my direction of travel.

When the first grey light of day awakened me there

was still a chill in the air. I slid into my boots after shaking them out. After a quick look around from atop that small cliff I stoked up my fire and heated a breakfast of coffee and a piece of smoked venison I had in my saddlebags. It was a welcome meal after a long day in the saddle and a good night's sleep. Once the sun broke it looked to be a beautiful day. It never ceases to amaze me how quickly the weather out here could change from bad to good, or for that matter, good to bad. After packing up my camp and concealing signs of my stay, I filled my canteen with lake water and rode carefully the six or seven miles to Pajarita Mountain.

If I did have anyone on my trail I needed to know. It was also important after pushing my horse as I had these past few days, for him to have a good rest and maintain his condition. I hobbled him in a small grassy meadow near the base of the mountain where there was a natural tank of runoff water collected from the storm. My day was spent dozing in the shade of some pinion trees, just far enough up the mountain to give me a good view of the country I had carefully ridden through the day before. If anyone was coming after me I might catch a glimpse of them crossing a ridge, or some smoke if they were stupid enough to build a fire without good cover.

One thing I noticed right off was that this piece of country sure was pretty. The trees sort of thinned out as you look down off the mountain toward the southeast, giving way to grassy areas in the canyon bottoms and rockier terrain on top of the rolling hills. Often there were sheer cliffs one hundred feet or more high where the torrential rains from storms like I'd been through the day before had swelled the streams into raging rivers, wearing away at the rock over time. The different rock and dirt forming the sides of those cliffs made the color vary from pale grey to a reddish brown, sometimes looking like a huge quilt hanging from a washline. There were several different cactus out there like prickly pear, cholla, and some varieties I'd never heard of back in Georgia. There were Yuccas five or six feet tall, with the stalk and flowers going up from there, extending toward the sky like so many Georgia Pine back east. The sky was an absolutely spotless blue, not showing any signs of the menace and anger that were all around yesterday. Rain from the storm made the colors even more striking and clean than they normally are. Yes sir, this high desert sure was pretty country.

Looking north about twenty miles I could see the Sierra Capitan mountains. The Indians called this mountain range the sleeping maiden because of it's silhouette. The mountains run east and west, and looking at them from the south as I am, you could see plainly how they got their name. The outline of the Capitans looks very much like that of a reclining woman, her waistline being Capitan Pass. My family was through that pass, waiting for me to come home to the ranch I'd located and helped build. Bill's place is on the north side of the Capitans, just west of the pass and along Carrizo Creek. We'd come out here together all of ten years ago, two years after the war ended. Our sister joined us and lives at Bill's ranch, in a separate smaller cabin near the main house.

Our father had been killed in the last days of the war, caught trying to work his fields by some union soldiers. He showed his anger at what they'd done to the land and was killed for it. Mom passed on a year and a half later, still missing Dad. That's when Bill and I decided to head west. We'd spoken of it many times, but with Mom gone we were free to look for a more comfortable place to settle. Maryellen could join us as soon as we found the place.

North of Lincoln seemed like as good a place as any. Lincoln had two stores, and White Oaks was fairly close and growing. Roswell off to the east was building up too. There were several places within a few days ride, but the ranch itself was located out of the way and seemingly in the wilderness. Once we built the ranch house, Bill's family followed, along with Maryellen. We built her cabin with logs from trees taken from the base of Sierra Capitan, just as Bill and I had done for the main house and barn. But with my brother's two sons helping when we built Maryellen's cabin we had more hands to lighten the load. The boys were just 12 and 16 years old, Luke being the elder. Both boys were healthy and lean, with a look that suggested they would grow tall. I hoped everyone was alright. It was my way to travel a lot, and wire Bill my whereabouts whenever I rode into a town. That way if there was a need for him to pass on any news he'd know how to contact me. Just one week ago I received a telegram asking me to come back to the ranch and help him. There was trouble of some sort brewing in the area and he'd like me to be there in case it ended up involving the family. I left that afternoon, heading northeast out of Texas with the intention of taking longer than I'd like to arrive, but using a different route than would be expected if anyone had it in mind to lay waiting for me along the way. It was in me to be watchful most all the time, but when headed for trouble I rode careful, suspecting trouble just to be safe. I suppose that practice came from the years I spent in the cavalry, and the war.

In between the catnaps I took all day I'd look back in the direction I'd come, trying to catch some sign of those following. I also had time to think about the camp I'd ridden through and the men who had been doctoring the brands on those horses. I wondered if they were part of the trouble Bill and I wanted to stay out of. Things had happened so quickly I doubted the man I'd run down had gotten a good enough look to know me if our paths crossed again. I'd not been looking for trouble, but those men gave it to me without a moment's hesitation. My reaction was pure reflex, doing what I knew best. Hunting trouble was no more my way than running from it.

The war between the states was not a time I had enjoyed, for we were all Americans, with no real enemy involved. There were times I did enjoy it in a way, but most of it was inconvenience. The inconvenience of not having enough of anything. Not enough time to get someplace, not enough food, not enough sleep, and not enough logistical support. The times I really felt alive were in the heat of battle, since I had been conditioned for it since youth. There was a stable not far from town owned by a former cavalry instructor. He was somewhere in his sixties and I'd stop on my way to and from town just to watch him work his horses. His name was Mr. Long, and somehow we became friends. He taught me how to ride those fancy stepping war horses, and to shoot from the saddle. Mr. Long showed me how to fight from a horses back, for he said sometimes being fair and in the right was not enough. Sometimes trouble would be forced onto a man, and in those times you must fight brutally but with a cool head and no hesitation. I think my old friend sensed something in me that I'd yet to see myself. As long as I live, my actions will be tempered with memories of Mr. Long, his lessons, and his way of preparing for dangerous times. Whenever I ride careful, my old teacher rides by my side, guiding me still.

Just after sundown, but still before the day lost any light, I spotted some smoke way off to the east. If that were the rest of the boys I'd had a run-in with, they were too far off my trail to be following me. Either they'd lost my sign or were more concerned with being identified as those who were stealing Chisum horses. Whoever they were, they were either in too big a hurry to stop early in the day, or were traveling long days and trying to conceal their fire by not starting it until after sunset. Either way, they were in the wrong direction to be following me. The only reason I'd been able to see their smoke is that it rose high enough just after sun set to be out of the shadow cast by the western horizon. There the sun lit it up like a pale whisper of a beacon. Tomorrow I'll take a round-a-bout way toward Lincoln, and see what news I can pick up before folks start seeing me with my family. I figured those that did not recognize me might speak a little more freely than if they could place me with a particular ranch in the area.

The stomping of my horse awakened me as the first rays of sunlight broke through the trees. Tom was eager to be on the move again after a welcomed day of rest. Before moving, I could see the birds flitting from branch to branch, and hear other normal animal noises. It relaxed me because if they were not alarmed there was probably no immediate danger in the area. I shook out my boots and stomped them on. After rising slowly, my Winchester in hand, I checked the area for anything out of place. Then with a shirt pocket full of dried venison I saddled up and rode the five miles west to Whitetail Mountain where I got down for a rest and a look around. I mounted and rode north again, keeping west of Pajarita Flats so the trees would conceal me and I could hide my tracks somewhat. After the flats I looked east to Dead Horse Hill, and moved on to water at the Rio Ruidoso. All had been quiet today, no sign of anyone tracking me and while I had seen some sign of shod horses I'd not sighted any people. After crossing the river I skirted Fox Cave, a popular camp site, not wanting to see anyone if I didn't have to.

Riding back into the rough country I split the difference between Devil's Canyon and Hightower Mountain, planning to camp along eagle creek. There were several places within easy riding distance but I'd camp in a secluded spot I knew where there was grass and water for my horse, it wasn't likely I'd run into anyone. I was surrounded by the settlements of Lincoln, San Patricio and Fort Stanton but it was rough and rocky terrain, much more difficult to travel than Devil's Canyon which was the usual path taken through these particular hills. My camp was soon enough after the climb to be appreciated, and just far enough to let my mount cool off a little before stopping. Scouting around before dark was my way, and I picked up enough wood to build a small fire after it got dark. It was very quiet here, except for the trickle of Eagle Creek and Tom's cropping of grass. I slept well, and woke early. Today I'd eat a real lunch in Lincoln, and make it to the ranch in time for supper. Hot coffee

warmed the September chill from my bones and I
headed out. I was anxious to be on my way for after
nearly two years, it would be good to see family again.

We made good time that morning, keeping east of
Fort Stanton and joining the road into Lincoln from the
west, near Priest Canyon. That spot offered a good
view of the road in each direction, and when I got
down onto the road there was enough cover for me to
conceal my tracks without being seen. Anyone trying
to track me would find only the sign in the road, and
not see where I'd come in from the brush. That way
they should figure I'd come east from the Rio Grande
and not be able to place me in the area of that shooting
trouble before the storm. I rode past Murphy's store
since Dolan was likely to be there and it had been his
brand going onto those horses. Past John Tunstall's
store was the Wortley Hotel. Word was they put on
some good meals so that is where I stopped for mine.
It was a tad early for lunch, but that way I could choose
my table and see who came in before they saw me.
Maybe I could even hear some talk from the other
tables and get a feeling of the situation in town. The
food was good, a big helping of roast beef, with a side
of potatoes and carrots. The carrots were tasty and
after commenting on them to the waitress I was told
they'd just been delivered the day before from a farm
further east along the Rio Bonito.

The waitress, Amanda, was friendly and since
there were no other customers I coaxed her to sit down
and talk a bit. I figured she would know as much about
any trouble as anyone else in town, perhaps more.
Turns out there was a good bit of tension building, but
no shooting trouble yet. Seems Tunstall's store was
taking some of Murphy's business and Murphy did not

like that even a little bit. Tunstall was trying to make money, like everyone and was selling his merchandise at competitive prices. He also had a little ranch south a ways, along the Rio Felix. The ranch was not a big operation, just a start. John Tunstall was friendly with the Mexican population as well as those on good terms with John Chisum, who everyone knew. Chisum has a ranch headquartered at South Spring near Roswell, but runs about 50,000 head of cattle along the Pecos from Fort Sumner down to Texas. Mr. Murphy had a different angle on things.

Murphy's partner, Jim Dolan, had a ranch along the Pecos near Seven Rivers, and was operating in loose association with the Beckwiths. Old man Beckwith had been a confederate who'd abandoned sizeable holdings near Lincoln and fled from the Union, only to return years later with nothing. Word around the valley was that the Beckwiths and some others, were making money selling Chisum's beef from time to time. The law in Lincoln, sheriff Brady, was friends with the Murphy bunch.

Amanda had told me enough about the situation for me to plan on keeping clear of the Murphy crew for a while, because of my recent shooting. I left the hotel on good terms with Amanda, and even left a decent tip on the table. After tying my horse up in front of Tunstall's store, I went inside to see what things he had in stock. It was a typical frontier store, with dry goods, food stuffs, and hardware. I bought some hard candy and sat on a wood bench outside after feeding Tom a piece of candy. Sitting there in the shade letting the candy dissolve in my mouth as I looked around it was hard not to notice just how pretty this town was. The Rio Bonito valley was narrow here, ice trees and thick grass sloping up into the hills within a few hundred yards from the back of each building. It would be nice here if there were no trouble. But now I needed to head for the ranch so my brother could give me the whole story.

It was now just passing twelve noon and there were but nine hours of light left in this early September day. I started west out of Lincoln, staying on the road for several miles to make good time. South of Capitan Pass I turned to the northwest. Rather than using the pass and coming up to Bill's place with the setting sun in my face, I'd go around West Mountain and approach from the south. We watered crossing the Rio Bonito, and at Jacob Spring made another stop. The water was cool and welcome. Letting Tom graze a few minutes I brushed off my clothing so I'd not be covered with quite so much dust when I rode up to the house just a few miles away. My brother would not mind the dust, but I wished to be presentable for my nephews. They'd not seen me in over a year and I'd not want them thinking poorly of me without cause. In Aragon Creek I washed up a mite, then stopped for a moment on the rise to enjoy the view of the ranch.

They'd done a lot of work in the past year or so, added two corrals and a round pen for the horses. A new hay barn sided one of the corrals with a half dozen foaling stalls. It looked like Bill was doing well with plans to build a reputation as a horse trainer. My shadow was long as I approached the house. First to see me was my sister, heading for the main house from her own with a big pot of stew. She called and everyone came out to welcome me. Bill and Sarah came from the main house with their new baby I'd not laid eyes on before this moment. Brushing hay from their shirts, Luke and Matt came from the new hay barn, running toward me with big smiles on their faces. Yes sir, it was nice having a family to come home to.

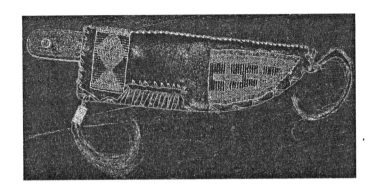

CHAPTER TWO

Supper that evening took a long time to eat, mostly since we were busy talking a good bit of the time. Everyone was doing well and all were healthy, even Katie, the new baby. As I figured by the looks of the ranch when I rode up, Bill was making a good go of it dealing horses to local anchers, and even to the government at Fort Stanton from time to time. He was becoming better known in the area for having good steady horses for sale at reasonable prices.

The boys were getting big, and Luke was developing into a farrier of sorts. He had taken to visiting the blacksmith in White Oaks whenever they went into town, Jake Martin, the smithie was teaching him some of the finer points of horses' feet. One day a week Luke worked preparing hooves for shoeing, a job which Jake would do himself. He'd also get other jobs ready so Jake could finish things a bit faster than when working by himself. This gave Luke a little money to put away, and helped the family by lessening Bill's dependence on a farrier for normal hoof maintenance. Matt was just a little behind Luke in size, and was a big help to my brother around the ranch, especially when they had new horses about the place. I'd picked up belt knives for each of the boys, trading with some Navajos a month or so back up the trail. After we finished eating I fished them out of my saddlebags and gave them to the boys. They were nice knives, crafted from the blade of a single draw-knife and nearly alike as two peas in a pod. Stag horn handles and copper guards were fitted onto each tang from both ends of the draw knife after it was straightened and fashioned into two separate blades. The sheaths were beaded and fringed, obviously crafted by Indian hands. A good knife was priceless in this country, and necessary in everyday life. I could tell my nephews were impressed with the knives, and would wear and use them with pride. It gave me a good feeling to see the looks on the boys faces as they strapped on their new treasures and repeatedly examined the blades.

Turns out Maryellen was engaged to Howell Hollis, a fellow we knew from back in Georgia. He had built a cargo ship and made some money ferrying goods along the coast. Now he was going to sell the ship and try his hand at overland shipping with a freight company he'd start out here. That way he'd be in a business he knew, and also be able to marry my sister and not take her away from the family. Howell's family had been killed in the war also, and he wanted to make a fresh start as badly as did we. The cabin they'd built had his touch, for he'd come out to propose marriage and help build their home. Now Howell was back east finalizing the deal to sell his ship. Planning on a family, they'd built the cabin with two separate bedrooms, I'd sleep in the spare for the time being.

Tomorrow would be a relaxing day around the

ranch. Bill and the boys wanted to give me a tour of the new barn and show me the horses. It would also give me a chance to find out the whole story behind Bill's request for me to return to our new home. Maryellen's cabin was built solidly, and I slept soundly in the first bed since I'd left El Paso.

That morning I woke with the first hint of light pushing through the window and between the curtains. As much as I enjoyed the sleep, I wanted to be up and about early enough to see what sort of routine my brother and the boys had. Once out on the porch I had just barely checked the horizon before Luke emerged from the main house, stretching with a yawn and pulling up his suspenders. He noticed me right away and waved a cheery greeting as Matt joined him from inside the house. Bill came out also, and the four of us headed for the well. Matt pumped a fresh bucket of cool water and carried it to the house where Sarah and Maryellen would soon be preparing breakfast. Bill smiled, showing me a hole in the side of the water trough just below the top. He'd rigged a drain pipe as an overflow for the trough, and it fed into a shallow ditch running to the corral. Bill kept working the pump and I followed the flow of water to another water trough partially buried at the edge of the corral where the horses could reach water but couldn't walk in it. Horses hitched to the outside of the corral at that spot could also drink. The durnedest part was that Matt had thought the whole thing up to make watering the horses easier. Now, instead of carrying buckets of water to the corral each day, all he has to do is work the pump handle until enough water makes it to the corral.

While Luke forked out hay for the horses, Bill and I walked around the corral giving each horse a check

for new injuries and a friendly rub on the forehead.
They had 16 head of mixed stock. All of them had a
good build, strong legs, straight backs, and looked to be
alert and smart. Bill said he didn't much care about the
breed of a horse as long as he had a good disposition,
was healthy, and looked to be smart with no meanness
in him. He had a couple paints and appaloosas, one
palomino, three roans, three bays, four blacks and one
buckskin. Most all of them were spoken for and the
oldest was 4 years old. Tomorrow Bill and Matt would
take the bays and blacks over to Fort Stanton and the
army, I'd go with them. It would be a two day trip,
travelling easy enough to deliver the remounts in good
shape.

Bill and I walked out from the corral a ways, and he
told me what it was that made him believe there was
trouble brewing in the region. He'd heard things in his
dealings with folks all over the area. Every one of us
knew Chisum's cattle were being rustled by several of
the small ranchers. Hugh Beckwith was headquartered
at Seven Rivers and was the original member of the
crew. But he was sided with his near neighbor, Jim
Dolan. The Murphy-Dolan store in Lincoln was the
den of these wolves, who were becoming more open
about trying to torment or scare away any customers
shopping at John Tunstall's store. Tunstall on the other
hand, was friends with the Chisum crowd and the local
Mexicans. Whenever his travels took him through
Lincoln, Bill would stop at Tunstall's store for any little
supplies they needed. He plain did not like dealing with
the roughnecks at The House (Murphy–Dolan store),
the store keeper and customers at Tunstall's were much
more friendly. With the rustlers becoming more
brazen, the time would come when Chisum would have

to do something about them. Bill figured that since he dealt mostly with Tunstall's store, even though he had not sided with either faction, the Murphy crowd would probably think him to be sided against them. Bill's ranch being close to Lincoln yet out of Chisum's normal range would be an easy mark for the rustlers if things got bad. Range wars could be mighty ugly and I was glad to be here with the family just in case. I offered to ride along whenever Luke or the others went away from the ranch, hoping my presence might help keep the vultures away. This would leave either Bill or me at home in case of trouble.

We heard Maryellen ringing the cowbell from the porch, our signal breakfast was ready.

"Haven't heard a bell like that since Ma's before the war." I said.

"It's the same bell." Bill replied smiling, "Maryellen found it in Ma's things after she died."

We headed for the house and the waiting flapjacks, bacon and biscuits. It was sort of like old times.

After the meal, Matt and Luke went about their chores while Bill and I walked a couple hundred yards from the house. Having been here scouting the area and building the main house, I knew the layout of the surrounding terrain, and the shortest routes when going to town. What I didn't know was how much the area had filled in. Why there were several cow camps between Lincoln and Roswell that had not been there before, and the area I'd come through when that hail storm hit is where the Seven Rivers crowd brings some of their stolen stock for branding! I reckon they just weren't used to having honest folks ride in unannounced! The boys, Bill and I decided to go for a ride, so we packed a bait of food and headed west for a few miles before cutting north toward Read Mesa. Once we got into some shade trees we swung back to the east, watering at Jacob Spring. Bill wanted to work some of the new horses once more before taking them to Fort Stanton tomorrow, just to make them more manageable on the trip. Since we were on the trail, everyone was wearing a pistol and had a saddle rifle. Luke and Matt each had Colt Navy revolvers that had been converted to chamber .38 colts, Bill wore an Army model 1860 converted to .44 colt. My pistol was a fairly new Peacemaker in .44 and the carbine in my scabbard was a new Winchester, also in .44. I favor large calibers for some chores so I had a second rifle, this one a Remington Rolling Block in 45-70 gvt. Bill's rifle was the Henry he'd brought back from the war, and the boys each had a Spencer carbine in .52. We weren't looking for trouble, but in this country it's just natural for a man to have something to protect himself and his kin with.

Just as we were thinking about mounting up and heading for the ranch, Matt spotted some deer a few hundred yards off and figured we needed more meat for the family. He'd heard from Bill that I favored rifles, and asked if I could hit a deer from here and save us the time of stalking in for a closer shot. Well my Remington takes to this type of shooting and it's exactly what I keep it around for. Sometimes you need to make a longer shot if you're gonna eat, and the carbines just don't cut the mustard for longer shots. Now I pulled out the rifle and slipped around the ridge following Matt, with Luke and Bill behind me. I calculated the distance at a mite over 300 yards and set the tang site accordingly, then laid on the edge of a little hollow and rested the rifle. When I fired, the doe had just put her head down to graze. She just jumped straight up and fell dead when that big slug hit her behind the shoulder. The other deer ran off, and the boys were just smiling and shaking their heads. Bill and I went back for the horses while Luke and Matt went to butcher the deer. I was glad for two things. First we had some good meat for the table. Second, I'd have been mighty embarrassed to disappoint those boys. By the time we got up there with the horses, the deer was about dressed. We tied her on behind Matt before heading for the ranch. We rode up to the ranch yard just as the sun began touching the horizon, and it took Luke almost no time at all to skin and quarter the deer carcass as Matt put up their two horses. Bill and I took care of our gear and horses, then headed for the house. Matt was a hand at stretching hides and he tacked this one up in the short time it took Luke to hang the deer quarters from the rafters in the barn. They knew what had to be done and took care of business without waiting to be told. Dinner would be ready shortly and they didn't want to miss out on a good meal like they knew would be waiting inside the house.

After a nice meal we all sat around on the porch visiting a while before Bill and I put the gear together we would need for tomorrow's ride to Fort Stanton. We went to sleep anxiously for the next day would start early and we were needful of sleep after the ride we'd had this day.

CHAPTER THREE

We woke early and after a quick breakfast of coffee and biscuits were in the saddle. Leading the army remounts off to the south just as the first gray light of day began taking over from the night, Bill was leading the four blacks, and Matt had the three bays. I rode my own horse, and whenever we approached difficult or suspicious terrain I rode out in front of the others, sometimes quite a ways. We headed south, and just as the sun topped West Mountain watered briefly at Jacob Spring. There was fresh elk sign there, and although it was still early in the day, it was too late to see elk out in the open, especially when making as much noise as we were. We pressed on wanting to make good time, and were alternating gaits between walking and a fast lope. Reaching the Rio Bonito west of Lincoln, near where I'd crossed when riding in from Texas, we stopped for a bite of the lunch Maryellen and Sarah had packed for us. We'd traveled quickly that morning and could afford the time, so we took an hour's rest to keep us fresh and cool the horses. We only had about four miles to go before delivering the horses and wanted to arrive in mid afternoon. The horses were in good condition and ready to continue, but with cool water and rich grass they did not mind lingering on.

Matt was excited at taking the trip with his father and I, for it took him away from the ranch and had him doing a man's work. After checking with Bill, I had promised my nephew a stay at the Wortley Hotel in Lincoln, and that probably had more than a little to do with Matt's excitement. We tightened our cinches and saddled up, continuing toward Fort Stanton. Finishing the first leg of our trip in good time and with no mishaps, by late afternoon we had concluded business at the fort and started for Lincoln. We left the fort riding northeast on the road to Lincoln. Looking for a quick and easy ride we decided to stay on the roads rather than cut our own trail in a more direct but time consuming route. It was not a busy day on the road, and we saw no one until reaching Lincoln.

After passing a few adobe rancheros we rode slowly past Murphy's store and the hard looks of two drifters standing on the front steps. One of those men was the man I'd run down in Crooked Canyon. We rode on to the hotel, they had a livery stable out back and we made that our first stop. After putting up the horses we brought our gear to the front desk of the hotel to get a room or two. I could see Amanda across the dining room bringing food to some of the few early evening customers. The clerk had bought a horse from Bill a couple months before, and he was right friendly. The hotel had a half dozen empty rooms and that clerk made us a good deal on three of them so we could each have our own bed. Matt was looking forward to a peaceful sleep in a new bed and was pleased with the arrangement. We all dusted off our clothes and took turns at the bathtub before meeting in the dining room for supper. There were several more folks having dinner now, and two of them were those drifters from Murphy's porch. We sat at a table in the back where I could see the drifters, and ordered steak and potatoes for each of us. Amanda remembered me, and recognized Bill from seeing him around town a few times. Matt was surprised that being the one from out of town it was me who made the introductions. After eating we took our coffee on the front porch. It was a long porch, the entire length of the hotel and had some wooden high-backed chairs for the hotel guests. We sat there in dim light from the dining room windows, enjoying a quiet evening and the peaceful feeling after a good meal.

Back in the livery I had told Bill who the one drifter was, so when the two of them came out and looked us over on their way past he knew why. Matt caught the looks but did not know the reason for them. I felt he'd be better off not knowing about that shooting just now. It was a sure bet that drifter would figure out where he knew me from someday. Seeing me with my brother and nephew was probably confusing him, for I was riding alone in the canyon that day. Perhaps we would make it out of town before it came to him who I was and he'd forget. After setting on the porch for a while we headed to our rooms and a good night's sleep.

In the morning we took our time getting out of bed, and were back in the dining room for breakfast after the rush was over. Being the only ones there we had a nice private breakfast of eggs and bacon. Amanda visited with us for a few minutes while the food was being prepared, but returned to the kitchen and dishwashing while we ate. After paying for the meal we picked up our gear from the corner and went out back to saddle up. The horses had survived the night inside the barn well enough and were ready to leave when they saw us come in. We mounted and rode over to Tunstall's store for a few odds and ends before heading back to the ranch.

As we rode past the torreone it was hard not to notice those same two drifters sitting in the stone tower's shade watching us go by. It was obvious they were waiting for us, but the looks on their faces were quizzical. I did not believe they knew it had been me at the branding fire that day, but now I was positive it was just a matter of time until they figured it out. We were riding abreast of each other, with me in the middle. I kept looking forward but spoke softly, just loud enough that my two partners could hear.

"Matt, I know the one with the big cut on his cheek but he doesn't remember me yet. On my way up here last week I rode into his camp looking to wait out a storm. He and his partner started shooting right off. I ran him down and shot his partner, that cut on his face is from my boot. They brought it to me, I had no choice. When he figures out who I am there will be trouble. After we finish in the store we'll ride east, right past them and out of town. We can swing back to the ranch after a while. If there's any trouble both of you stay wide of me."

There was no more talk until we went into the store. Bill knew the score, he'd been in more than a few scrapes during the war. With a little luck Matt could wait to learn, I'd rather not take a chance on him getting hurt. Bill went about his business picking out some fabric Sarah wanted and something for the baby. Matt was looking at hardware, probably with some other project in mind like the water trough back at the ranch. I picked up a box of 44's and two of 45-70 cartridges, not wanting to get caught short if there was trouble. After paying for our merchandise we stepped onto the porch outside, and there were our troublesome friends. The one with the cut was looking at my horse and outfit, the other was a few feet behind the big morgan. After nodding for Bill and Matt to mount up, I advanced to my horse, brushing past the drifter. He watched me put the cartridges in my saddlebag then stood between me and my reins. As I moved toward the reins he slipped them from the hitching post. Handing them to me he said:

"Expectin' trouble mister?"

"Always do." I replied. "Thanks for keeping an eye on my horse."

"I believe I've seen you around." Said the drifter.

"It's a small world, maybe I've seen you and just didn't take notice." I said.

I mounted quickly and backed up, nearly stepping on the other man before swinging east and riding out of town with Bill and Matt. We were quiet. Bill and I were listening and I could tell Matt wanted to speak but was holding back for now. After a few minutes when we were clear of town, he at last spoke up.

"Is he one of the men stealing Mr. Chisum's cattle?"

"Don't know." I answered. "But he steals horses. They were branding some of Chisum's when I rode in. I figure that's why they just started firing without even a howdy."

"What do you think he'll do if he remembers you?"

"Not if, Matt, but when." I kept speaking. "He will remember sooner or later, otherwise he'd not be dogging me now. If it comes to him quick enough he might come after us. If he's too slow in his thinking there may be other folks around and he'd tell them too. I'd just as soon not have a bunch of them come after me at once. Let's swing around to the north, there's a spring at Pierce Canyon we can water at."

As we started turning from the road I noticed two riders coming up a few hundred yards behind us. It was the two drifters riding side by side, coming in at a fast lope. We had company after all. Matt had just turned off the road and Bill was behind me. I let Matt keep riding and told Bill to stay to my right, just off the road. Matt was now about forty yards further and I called for him to stop, but stay there. I figured he was far enough away these drifters would think him to be out of the fracas. I removed the thong from my pistol before turning my horse around to face the southwest, putting my right side toward the two riders who were just now pulling up and continuing toward us at a walk. I sat my horse and waited to see what their intentions were.

They were talking quietly to each other as they

rode up, too quiet for us to hear. When they got to be about thirty yards away the one I'd spoken with angled his horse toward my brother and the other rider split to my left. This attempt to gain a superior position told me what I needed to know. I walked my horse forward toward a rock outcropping near the road's edge cutting him off from continuing around behind me. Then I turned toward them slightly and moved forward, causing the one nearest me to stop about ten yards away. The other stopped the same distance from Bill, directly in front of him. That put him about fifteen yards from me. I noticed the man near me had the holster thong removed from the hammer of his pistol. Every man out here in the west kept that thong over the hammer to keep his gun in the holster, unless he was expecting to need it. When I looked at the talkative one he was just turning his head from Bill's direction to look at me. His holster was empty and his right hand on the saddle horn. I could just see the butt end of his pistol underneath the left side of his open coat. The pistol was tucked into his pants with the grip just a couple of inches from his right hand, and Bill could not possibly see it from his angle. So this was it, he'd make the first move by shooting my brother, the other would shoot me as I drew on the first man. My right hand rested on my thigh and I could feel the hammer of my colt pushing lightly on the underside of my forearm.

The man from the rustler's camp spoke first, with the slow steady voice of a man who's been here before. His eyes told me of the hatred he felt.

"You're the one killed Bob down to Crooked Canyon, and you ran me down too."

"There was a storm brewing and I was just looking for a place to wait it out." I countered. "You fella's started shooting before you knew what I was about."

"Makes no nevermind to me." He scowled angrily."You killed Bob and now I'm going to kill you and......"

His fingers loosened their grip on the saddle horn so he could reach for his hidden gun. I drew smoothly and fired once just as he jerked the pistol from his pants. My bullet caught him in the right chest just in front of the bicep, angling crossways through the middle of his chest. As I brought my gun to bear on the one near me his pistol was just clearing it's holster and I fired again, hitting him square in the chest. Both men fell from their saddles as Bill drew his pistol. Matt sat his horse, calmly regaining control of the spooked animal. Bill looked at the two gunmen and holstered his pistol. Had I not noticed the holsters and hidden gun it would be Bill and I lying in the dust, and perhaps even Matt. I reloaded the empty chambers in my pistol, putting the empty casings in my pocket so they wouldn't be found. Bill spoke first.

"Now they'll be after us for sure, it's too bad he recognized you."

"You and Matt go on up to the spring and wait for me, don't make too much dust." I said. "I'll tidy up here."

Their horses were nervous with the smell of blood in the air, but had not run off. I quickly gathered up the reins and tied them to trees behind the rock outcropping. The drifters' bodies I drug behind the rocks and left with pistols at hand as if they had been laying in ambush for someone coming along the road. Then I hurriedly brushed out tracks and other sign in the road, sifting dirt over it all. Needing to leave before anyone had time to get out here from town, I mounted Tom and rode through the trees toward Pierce Canyon. I stayed off the trail for a while, not wanting to leave fresh tracks or kick up any dust. Hopefully, anyone coming from town to investigate the shots would ride on past covering any sign I'd left with their own and not finding the dead men until returning to town. If they did not look too closely, it might seem as if the men were killed in an ambush they had set for someone else.

When I came to the clearing around the spring, Bill and Matt rode out into the open. After watering their horses they had retreated into the shadows just beyond the tree line so they could see anyone coming up the trail before being seen themselves. They had their rifles in hand in the event that I was being pursued. Bill was serious and alert, the old soldier in him coming out once more. Matt looked nervous, his eyes wide with excitement. Though he'd not been near anything like this before now, he knew what might need to be done and would follow his dad's lead. It's a hard country out here with hard people. Sometimes good men need to defend themselves from evil. That can't always be done without violence. A man's got to be observant and alert for trouble, and willing to do whatever it takes to survive.

We stayed long enough to water my horse and rode on. Following a game trail in the trees along the southern base of Sierra Capitan, we worked our way westward toward the pass. Keeping under the trees we would remain hidden even from a distance, and any dust we kicked up would also be concealed. Trying to make up for the time lost in taking a roundabout route we pushed the horses a little and after crossing the pass stopped at Gum Spring just after noon. It had been a hard ride through rough country and we were all glad to rest and let the horses drink.

As the horses lazily grazed, we ate the beef sandwiches Amanda had prepared for us back at the hotel. I had not had the chance to speak with Matt since the shooting and it was he that spoke up first.

"Uncle, that drifter moved first and you still beat him. Then you got the other one too. I didn't know you could shoot like that."

I thought for a moment and replied, "Matt, generally speaking killing is not good, but sometimes it has to be done. I've never started trouble, but when it's brought to me I try to plan as best as I can. When the time comes it has to be fast, without hesitation. When I saw them coming I knew there would be trouble so your father stayed off to the side just far enough that we could move if need be. We slipped the thongs from our hammers just to be ready. When those men rode up I kept them both in front of us and noticed one had the thong off his hammer too and the other had an empty holster, his pistol tucked into his pants under his coat. His hand was close to the gun and I figured him to make the first move, his partner to shoot me before I could get off a shot. I knew what was going to happen and what I needed to do. When he moved, he needed to grab the pistol from his pants and pull it out before coming up to shoot. All I had to do was sweep my pistol up to shoot, then cover the other man. When that one brought his pistol out I was already on him and it was a simple thing to stop him too."

"I understand you had to do it, but you made it look so easy." Matt said.

"Like I said Matt, they didn't know what we'd do but I knew what they were going to do. That made the difference. I was willing to stop them and had thought out exactly what I would have to do. You know I've been a lawman. I still ride on the side of the law, but that doesn't mean I'll be taken advantage of ."

Explaining what I did with the dead men and what I hoped anyone finding them would think, I told them we should keep news of this inside the family. The rest needed to know of it so they would be careful of outsiders, but if my set up worked, we didn't need to let the truth leak out. Bill was concerned that they'd follow us, and rightfully so. But I thought the ambush scene would slow them up long enough to have any sign I missed covered with new. By that time it would be too late to think anything else happened. It might even be some time before the men were found.

Bill spoke out. "We ought to just ride back to the ranch and go about our business normally, but be careful of anyone we see around. Nobody will expect to see us in town for a week or so, by then maybe no one will be concerned about this anymore."

We tightened up our cinchas and rode back to the

ranch. We still rode a mite carefully, but made good time and were home well before dark.

CHAPTER FOUR

Our family had expected us to return about midday, but were not overly concerned with our delay. We took care of horses and gear before calling everyone together at the main house. When Bill spoke of our shooting and the circumstances leading up to it, they were relieved we were unhurt. It was agreed we would keep the whole thing between the family rather than attracting unwanted attention by letting the Murphy crowd know who'd killed their men. When we finished the meeting, Luke walked away with Matt, talking quietly. I imagine Luke was getting Matt's side of the story.

For almost a week things went along normally at the ranch. Bill had been approached by John Chisum some time back about training horses for his "Jinglebob" outfit. They brought their cow horses from Texas, but had heard of my brother's work and wanted to see what he could do with a half dozen untrained mounts. It was about noon on Wednesday when two men rode in trailing six head of horses. It turned out to be Milo Pierce and Lou Paxton. They sometimes day worked for Chisum, and had a small outfit downstream from the spring where we watered our horses after the shooting. After corralling the horses we went to the house for lunch, giving the riders a nice break before they rode to Lincoln.

Pierce was a slightly built man with an unruly mustache and was much more talkative than his partner. It was common for visitors to inform ranchers of any news from town, and Milo was up to date on many things. The most interesting to us was news of the death of two men who had been seen lingering with the Murphy crowd. Seems they'd laid in ambush for someone heading east from Lincoln and been killed in their own trap. It was Milo and Louis that had found them on their way to Lincoln several days ago. After eating their share our visitors rode off, anxious to be in Lincoln before evening. They were expected in a card game with some other folks.

Thursday we just let the Chisum horses get used to being in a new place and looked them over. They were smaller built than many horses, and their mustang bloodlines were easy to see. Bill figured on waiting a few more days for the horses to settle down before starting to work on them. Since it was time once again for Luke to work at the blacksmith's, Bill would start on the horses when Luke and I returned from White Oaks.

At first light on Friday, Luke and I headed west for

Carrizo Canyon. We figured to make White Oaks by late morning, giving Luke most of the day to get some work done for Jake. It was a pleasant ride through open country until we made it into Carrizo Canyon. There the terrain started getting rougher as we climbed into the pines and hardwoods that covered Patos and Carrizo Mountains. We joined a pack trail that would lead us over the saddle of these two mountains into White Oaks Canyon and on into town. We stopped off the trail on the west side of the saddle to water the horses at Barber Spring. It was only a few more miles to town but we'd been pushing the horses a bit to make good time and the few minutes rest would do us all good. After the horses drank their fill we mounted up and started the easy downhill ride into town.

The town was really just a settlement set up less than two miles southeast of the Crenshaw ranch headquarters. There were three big ranches in the area and old man Crenshaw thought it would be convenient for all three if there were a supply point closer than Lincoln to the southeast or Dowlin's Mill yet further to the south. Just over a year ago Crenshaw convinced the other ranchers it would be a good thing for them too, and the three of them put up a wood frame building in White Oaks Canyon that would be a gift to whoever they could convince to set up a store there. A merchant headed west with goods heard about it in Lincoln and soon had decided that the building near Crenshaw's was as far west as he would get. Now there was a blacksmith, a small restaurant that served as a gathering place and saloon, and a few tents that belonged to prospectors who spent a day or two at a time up in the hills looking for gold . The saloon even had three spare rooms upstairs that were rented out from time to time, serving as sort of a hotel.

We rode up to Jake's shop and Luke started right in to work. Jake and I visited for a while and he seemed a likeable sort. After a bit I put my horse, Tom, in the corral out back of the barn and walked over to the mercantile to see if they had anything I could not do without. It was a small building with a covered porch and a sales floor that was crowded with merchandise. I supposed he'd stocked up enough to last him the winter if need be. They had a good selection of blue, gray and green flannel shirts. I bought a couple of new shirts, and a twelve gauge coach gun with buckshot that would be handy if anything happened back at the ranch. The clerk wrapped them all up for me in a bundle I could tie behind my saddle. After dropping the package off at Jake's near my saddle, I headed to the saloon for some lunch.

There were a few horses standing three legged at the hitching post in front of the store, enjoying the warm mid day sun. The saloon's front door was held wide open by a ladder-backed chair like I would probably find more of inside. There were two men sitting at a table over in a corner that looked darker than it really was since I had just come in from the sunlight. The aroma of fresh baked bread filled the room, covering the stale beer and tobacco odors normally overpowering the other smells. A third man standing at the bar turned and stared at me as I came in, following my progress until I leaned on the middle of the bar. A nod I gave him went unanswered and he joined the other two at the table. They had not even looked up, but I figured they knew a stranger was in the room. The bartender came out of the back and before moving to a table off to the side I agreed to a hot lunch of beef stew and bread. The man from the bar was sitting sideways with his two friends, staring at me with an inconvenienced look on his face. The other two were both good sized and solidly built, but still did not bother to look up. The bartender brought out my plate of stew along with the pitcher of water I'd asked for and set them on the bar. The man who'd been watching me stirred in his seat. As I got up and walked toward my food he also rose, sauntering toward me as if he was about to speak. I'm not a large man, standing just under six feet and a bit on the lean side. But I've seen my share of fighting and figured I was about to see more. I gathered the silverware and plate up in my left hand, reaching for the water with my right. This man was a hair over six feet tall and outweighed me by about thirty pounds. He pushed the pitcher away as I reached out, smiling like a child playing a prank on a smaller friend.

Looking him in the eye I spoke up. "Excuse the reach friend, I'd like my water."

I reached across his arm toward my pitcher and he moved his hand upward, brushing mine away from the handle. I set my plate back down on the bar as he spoke.

"Can't figure why a man would be in a saloon drinkin' water, just don't make no sense to me."

"It don't have to." I replied. "It's my water and I'll drink it with my food if I wish."

"Bartender!" He called out, slapping his open hand
down on the bar. "A couple 'a beers for me and my
new friend!"

He was facing me, with his right hand on the bar.
I grabbed the back of his hand with my right, and
twisted it hard, pulling to my right and down. The
troublemaker was thrown away from the bar and
sprawled to the floor. He turned and got half way to
his feet before I hit him with a left to the side of his
face that put him back on the floor, unconscious, a
trickle of blood appearing from the end of his nose.

Stepping away from the sleeping one I squared up
facing those two big men still sitting at the table. Even
though their faces were hidden they looked familiar.

"You two fellas have any irons in this fire?" I called out
loudly.

"No sir, not us!" they replied together, standing and
tipping back their hats as if on cue.

No pair of twins could look any more alike than
these two, and I knew them well. My old Compadres
from days as both soldier and lawman, Hank and
Frank! They were smiling and walked over to shake
hands.

Frank spoke first. "When we saw you walking up the
steps it looked like something would happen with you
and this fella Sam. He's been trying to impress us since
we met him yesterday."

"Yeah," Hank added, "so we figured to just let him play

out his hand on his own and kept quiet about knowing you. It turned out about like we figured it would."

After dragging Sam outside, the twins brought their drinks to my table. We visited as I ate my meal, and for quite a spell afterward. It had been a couple years since I'd seen them last. We first met during the war when they joined my unit temporarily while traveling back to their own unit. They had both been wounded bad enough to stay in the field hospital for several days. That was long enough to let their unit move to another location and they needed to travel a piece to catch up with them. They camped with us one night and since I was the Lieutenant they had to check in with me. When we went into battle the next day the twins rode with us and since it took a few days for the running engagement to end we had a chance to fight alongside each other. That's when I received a field promotion to Captain, just before Hank and Frank moved out to find their own unit again. It was about 5 years later when I was a town marshal in Arizona Territory and they came into town for some entertainment. A few cowpokes were stupid enough to start trouble with them and the twins set them straight without much trouble. When I found them finishing their drinks we recognized each other right off. Before a week went by they were both my deputies. After some busy times together the town quieted down too much to suit them so Hank and Frank moved on. Eventually I left too, and here we are bumping into each other once more.

Turns out the brothers had been riding through Lincoln two days ago and were approached by James Dolan at the Murphy-Dolan store as they bought some supplies. They are a couple of good hands in a fracas and Dolan wanted them to think about hiring on at his ranch down at Seven Rivers to the southeast. It was Sam's job to try and convince the twins to sign on. He wasn't doing such a good job and had ridden to White Oaks with them while trying to figure a way to get them to join up. As I finished my meal I told them of my family, the ranch, and the bit that I knew of what was going on in the area. They had been told of the two Murphy men found dead by the roadside near Lincoln as an example of why they should hire on with that crew. Knowing I could trust these two old friends I told them quietly how those men in the rocks had been killed. Hank and Frank were honest hands, and had not planned on signing with Murphy's bunch to begin with. Now they would not, and since they were just riding with no destination in mind would stay in the area a while in case trouble developed for me or my family.

About this time Luke came through the door. He'd brought our horses out and tied them in front of the saloon. It was late in the afternoon and time for us to head back to the ranch. Before heading out I introduced Luke to the brothers. Turns out Sam had gone to Jake's shop to have a loose shoe replaced on his horse before leaving town and was complaining about being thrown out of the saloon. Luke wanted to know what had happened and the twins surely had fun telling him the story. Before Luke and I headed out I told Hank and Frank how to get to the ranch. They'd be out in a day or so to meet the family and see how things were set up.

We had a pleasant ride home, much easier than the trip into town. After the short climb to Barber Spring it was all downhill to the plain. The moon was out early and bright, so it was a pretty sight when the ranch buildings came into view in the distance with the moon above and behind them.

CHAPTER FIVE

After Luke and I put up our horses and gear we walked to the main house and found Bill standing on the porch. He'd heard us ride in and came out to welcome us back home. My brother asked if there was trouble in White Oaks. In search of a snack after our ride I just told him I'd run into some old friends and if he came to the kitchen I could tell him over a quick bite to eat. Luke followed along looking for some food too.

We found some beef and bread in the kitchen and slapped together a couple of nice sandwiches. Bill asked again about White Oaks and I told him of Hank and Frank, letting him know we'd have friendly company soon. Figuring Luke would tell him about the scuffle, I excused myself and headed for Maryellen's house, and the spare room. Walking past the barn I picked up the gear I'd bought in town and walked up the steps into my sister's house. Quiet as I was she heard me enter and got up just to make sure it was me. After a quick sisterly hug she went back to her room and I to mine. Taking off boots and pants I climbed into bed wearing long johns, my rifle and pistol near to hand.

The morning started normally at the ranch, Bill and the boys tending the animals while Sarah and Maryellen prepared a meal. Joining in near the barn, I helped Matt inside for a time before checking on the horses with Bill. We roped a couple of the Chisum horses and tied them to the corral fence so they'd be calmed down a bit by the time we were done with breakfast. Luke had done the heavy work, moving some grain and a few bales of hay to where it would be easier to get to later in the day. The four of us headed for the house together, anxious for the food we could smell as we neared the house.

During breakfast we talked of the usual family things. Sarah was amazed at how small the world can be sometimes, what with me bumping into Hank and Frank while in White Oaks. They would be nice to have around, always happy and joking, but good hands and handy if there was to be trouble. While Luke and I were in White Oaks a messenger had ridden out to the ranch from Lincoln with a telegraph message for my sister. Maryellen's fiancé, Howell, had completed the sale of his cargo ship back east and was traveling west to set up a new business before officially joining the family. He'd made it as far as New Orleans before sending the wire.

Plans were that he'd have a cargo business carrying goods between Roswell, Lincoln, Dowlin's Mill and White Oaks. He hoped to pick up some army contracts at Fort Stanton and sometimes make trips to Sante Fe, as well as helping the family horse business improve by being an agent for Bill whenever he heard of someone looking for good horses. The fastest way to get here would be a train to El Paso and a stage headed north to Albuquerque might have a mail stop at Dowlin's Mill or even Lincoln. If that's his route he could be here inside of a week. It will be nice to have him in the area, especially for Maryellen. She's been anxious for Howell to relocate out here so they could start a family of their own.

We had a great breakfast of fresh biscuits and eggs, with some venison steak to help us last through the day. Bill planned to work more with the horses while the boys added to a new fence line for a second and larger corral to the north of the barn. I walked around near the barn and houses looking once more at how things were set up, then I settled into the swing seat on Maryellen's porch to think on a few things. Adding that fellow, Sam, from Dolan's store trying to recruit the twins to everything else that has happened it surely looks like that bunch is getting ready for something. Since the ranch was located in the open it would be hard to approach without being seen. Aragon Creek was to the south not quite four hundred yards from the main house, and in an arroyo that was sometimes deep enough to conceal a man on horseback. Just because we had no dogs in whatever fight lie ahead, doesn't mean folks would figure it that way. If ever there were an attack on the ranch there is a good chance that creek bed is where it would come from.

After my thoughts were fitted together more completely I started in with myself appointed chore for today. With Howell arriving soon and all the beds taken up I figured to make him a new one. He'd be staying nights in the main house until the wedding, but would be needing a bed until then. After the wedding I'd be the one needing a bed in the main house so I spent the rest of the morning picking through the cut trees Bill had stored in a pile near the round pen, looking for the straightest ones. The boys would cut fence posts from them as they were needed for the new fence, but I swiped a few for my project. The straightest ones would be for the platform with others supporting it from the floor. I'm no carpenter but I can build things from wood if I set my mind to it. When I finished it, the bed platform was two feet off the floor and level enough a thin mattress would make it mighty good for sleeping. Luke helped me carry it into one of the extra rooms in the main house where it would wait for Howell.

Some of the cut trees were a tad big around for fence posts and I spent the remaining sunlight cutting some of them into three foot long sections with a bow saw. Then I carried six of these sections to the corner of the main house which faces Maryellen's cabin and six more to the side of Maryellen's place which faces the main house. I had six more logs for the barn and needed another eighteen. Everyone was gathering for supper so I figured the cutting and moving I had yet to do could wait until tomorrow. After drawing some water from the pump I washed off and joined the others in the main house.

We had a good meal and not much conversation. All of us had worked most of the day and so were ready to relax. Bill had made some progress with the two horses we'd roped before breakfast and a few of the others as well. He still had a way to go but was pleased with how they were doing so far. Matt and Luke had added a dozen more fence posts to the corral and it now had two sides. If you've never used a pointed steel pole to break the soil up so you could dig it from a post hole you have no idea how hard the boys worked. We leaned back and enjoyed the full feeling after supper and talked of family things. Bill was curious about the short logs I'd cut and we adjourned to the porch so I could explain what I was up to.

If there was a paranoid member of the family it was me. But my suspicions had kept me alive in the past so I almost always minded my feelings. Looking at the two houses and the barn was like looking at three corners of a triangle, each building facing the other. The two small corrals were behind the barn with one common fence between the two and centered against the stalls so horses in each corral had shelter. The round pen was between the near corral and the main house, so if somebody working horses had a problem anyone in either the house or barn would know. I planned to build a low wall at the outside corners of each building so if the ranch came under attack people caught outside would have cover as long as the attackers were outside the perimeter of the buildings. The walls would be angled toward the nearest building so that even though they would provide cover for those of us inside them, those outside would be exposed to fire from the other buildings. We might never need them, but I was summoned here in case trouble developed and I did not plan on letting the family down if things went sour. Bill just looked me in the eye for a few moments as he lit his pipe. Then nodding his approval shook my hand saying that having me here was a comfort to him. We sat side by side on the porch steps for a time before the boys joined us in watching darkness swallow the landscape.

The next morning started as most others with the men doing their chores until called to breakfast. Again Bill and I roped and tied a couple of horses, the one he had not worked with the day before and another. The boys tended to their business, and then we all ate. When I went outside the boys followed. They had been told by their father to help me with the barricades. It was a pleasure to work with them for Luke and Matt really got down to business when there was a task at hand. Matt helped measure and cut the remaining logs as Luke harnessed a horse to an old travois, loaded the logs for us and dragged them to their positions. The work really went fast and by midday half of the barricades were complete. With stakes in place to hold the others we took a lunch break, planning to easily be finished before dark.

The remaining work was simply dropping logs into place between the stakes that would hold them on top of each other. We secured them by lashing together the top of the stakes on either side of the logs. The sun was half way down in the west as we completed everything. Luke was putting up the harness while Matt and I stood near Maryellen's cabin next to the last barricade, looking off in the distance. Matt was pretty sure he'd spotted some movement in the creek just below the sun. I sent him to slowly go to the main house in case we needed another gun. My colt was holstered and I loosened the thong as two riders emerged from the arroyo and Aragon Creek. It could

be the twins but with the sun in my eyes I couldn't tell
for sure. They rode straight in for about fifty yards
before turning north. Once they got out of the
glare from the sun I could tell it was Hank and Frank.
It would be just like them to examine the ranch from a
distance and come in from our most vulnerable
direction. I waved a greeting before they turned back
toward me and nudged the horses to a lope for the few
hundred yards remaining in their ride from White Oaks.

Still holding his Spencer, Matt stepped out onto
the porch after I called to him that all was well. The
twins came to a stop a few yards away from me and
dismounted together, walking the last few steps to our
handshake.

"Howdy boys, it's good to see ya."

"It's just like you, Captain, to spot us before we got into
range." Hank said with a smile.

Frank added pointing at Matt, "And then send
somebody for a long gun."

"Well now, you boys ought to know that creek is in
range of my rifle, and it wasn't me that spotted you, it
was my nephew, Matt."

Holding the rifle loosely in his left hand and
looking relieved, Matt walked up and I introduced him
to my friends.

"You're alright boy." Announced Hank with another
grin. "I reckon you'll do fine."

Matt was beaming, enjoying the compliment. Hank, a big, tough man, was speaking of Matt spotting them on his own and following my directions without question. No more could be expected of a grown man, and when he looked at me I smiled proudly giving him a nod of approval.

There isn't much that goes unnoticed on a small ranch such as this one. Before long The whole family knew of the twin's arrival and gathered in the middle of our small compound for introductions. Since everyone knew about each other it was like meeting old friends once again for all of us. I have strong bonds with family as well as my old compadres and each accepted the others immediately. With the sun getting low over Carrizo Mountain we decided to call it a day. Once the horses were tended to and gear stowed we gathered for our evening meal.

It was a comfortable table at supper that night even though with Hank and Frank among us there were a lot of bumping elbows. We stayed up late, with Luke, Matt and the women alike excited by stories of times long behind us. The twins were jovial and talkative by nature, only keeping quiet when better judgment and the situation commanded. They also enjoyed young folks and storytelling. With the boys curious about life outside of the ranch there were constant questions being thrown at Hank and Frank. It seemed as soon as they answered one question with a story there was another asked before they could catch their wind. My brother even learned a few things about me that I'd not spoken of before. There was some talk of the war since that's how I had met the twins, but soon there was talk of Arizona.

It was there, in the mining town of Sierrita that I

had been marshal for almost five years. Back in '70 I had just been marshal for a few months when Hank and Frank rode into town and joined up with me as deputies. With miners coming into town from the mountains to spend money they'd worked hard for, there were always people drifting in with an eye out for an easy stake. Mostly the regular town folks were peaceful and had businesses to run. There were a couple of hotels, three mercantiles, a restaurant (beside the hotel kitchens), and two stables. But the real draw was the four saloons with their girls and gambling. The town site is only a long day's ride south and west of Tucson, so many of the riff raff that are run out of there in a hurry head for Sierrita.

There was plenty of business for a lawman and the town marshal before me had been killed about two weeks before I rode into town. When I got there things were out of control, still no marshal and the town folk were afraid to leave their homes after dark. If they had to go out you'd see them scampering from shadow to shadow trying to keep out of sight. It was stories of this town that most interested my family, and the twins were primed and ready to tell some tales.

The evening flew by and before long we were turning up the lantern wick for a little more light while burning the midnight oil. The last story told that night explained to my family how I acquired matching Colt pistols. It had been quiet in town for almost a year and I had made mention to the town council that I might move on. It took me a couple of months to really decide and by that time the pistols had arrived. The council had ordered them, worried I might leave without a token of their appreciation for my work. They were nice pistols, nothing fancy just everyday peacemakers. But they were the newest pistols available, .45 caliber with five and a half inch barrels. Usually I only wore one but have been known to strap on the other pistol if it seemed the thing to do. I never did tell the family about it, but they knew now and looked at me with a different sort of glint in their eyes while saying goodnight, especially the boys.

CHAPTER SIX

The day started early at the ranch, no matter staying up late the night before. There were chores to do and the animals depended on my nephews and brother for regular attention. Nights were getting cooler as the season progressed and the usual heavy dew was now becoming frost on most mornings. It made a beautiful sight at dawn, with the sunlight sparkling off the frosty grass and the boulders on the side of Sierra Capitan. The view only lasts a short time each morning for once above the horizon the sun's heat could be felt almost immediately, melting frost and warming your bones from the chill.

As Bill and his sons did chores I collected my gear

and carried it to the barn in preparation for my ride to Lincoln. With Hank and Frank at the ranch it was easy to leave without worry for my family. Howell would be arriving soon, possibly this week and I wanted to be there when he arrived if possible. The family all knew where I was going and we had a busy conversation at the breakfast table. While I was in Lincoln, the twins would be riding the desert and mountains in a wide circle around the ranch for a couple or three days searching for any suspicious sign and learning the area. When they returned it would again be time for Luke to work in White Oaks, Hank would accompany him this time.

Maryellen packed a sack of food for me to take on the ride. She always gave me more than I needed, but in this country it's better to have a bit more than a bit less. If for whatever reason I didn't make Lincoln today, I'd need a little more than just today's lunch in my saddlebag. After leaving the ranch I rode southeast, cutting across the desert for Capitan Pass. It was the fastest way to Lincoln and it was my wish to be in town well before the dinner hour. The twins gathered their horses as I rode off, walking at first to loosen up Tom's muscles then stepping up to a lope. Making good time across the open ground I skirted under the looming mass of West Mountain. The openness of the high desert is deceiving and what appears to be flat and empty is actually made up of small rises and depressions one after the other, some of them deep arroyos cut by churning water from the many powerful storms sweeping across the west. Stopping briefly for water, I took a look around Gum Spring for any sign of man.

Someone had spent the night on a small bench eighty yards uphill from the spring, a large heavy man wearing boots. He rode one horse and led another that carried a pack. I could see the sharp marks the pack frame had made where it rested in the dirt overnight. When he'd bent over putting out his small fire something had lightly swept the ground, perhaps a long fringed buckskin shirt. If he had not brushed away tinder from around the fire I might not have noticed the sweep marks in the dirt. Whoever it was kept a tidy camp and carefully disguised his sign near the spring, but had not bothered to cover tracks around his camp. We were both headed in the same direction so perhaps I'd see him in town.

Leaving the spring we headed east on a trail widened with use by those passing through the gap for many years. The ground became extremely rocky and more difficult as we climbed further above the desert. Thick brush gave way to pines and rock slides, West Mountain being too steep and rough to climb along this route. Reaching the top of the pass I was heading south and dim trails came in from either side, down from the ridge back of Sierra Capitan. The soft warm breeze of mid day switched direction amidst the turmoil of the pass and Tom's ears perked up as his muscles stiffened underneath me. He'd picked up a scent that made him nervous. He perked up at most anything that caught his attention, and stayed that way for animals that we would pass. But men were a different story. Whenever we came across anyone unexpected he would also tense his muscles in preparation to move. I'd trained him as I'd been taught so many years ago before the war, and the effort payed off at times like these. Guiding Tom with knee pressure and almost imperceptible movements of the reigns, we eased slowly off the trail away from whoever it was that had him buggered. Stopping behind a large tree I considered for a moment what was likely happening. From time to time after leaving the spring I'd seen the tracks of the man at Gum Spring and had seen them just before Tom warned me of a stranger. There were a couple large boulders poking up between the heavy branches of some big pines thirty yards to the side and slightly above the trail. The flat top of one boulder was partially hidden by thick green branches and could easily conceal a man, allowing him to command the pass. He must be there watching. Neither of us could shoot the other and I was safe for the moment, but if I moved into the open it could mean my death.

Shucking my winchester from it's scabbard I held it across my legs and called out:

"Are we going to stay here all day or can I ride on in to Lincoln?"

"Ride on friend..." drifted down from the rocks, "...I'd rather have you in front of me than coming up my back trail like you've been."

Countering I replied "How about you slide down off that rock and we can ride into the open together. I'd rather keep somebody who'd lay waiting for me where I can see him."

We came to an agreement before meeting in the small clearing at the saddle of the pass. Turns out he'd seen me coming into the canyon near Gum Spring and covered his sign some before heading out. Tom's gait had me making better time than he was with his pack animal, so we were catching up to him. He'd been watching and decided to take a closer look at me before I got too close and put him at a disadvantage. "Bear" Hastings was a trapper spending most of his time in the Sacramento Mountains to the southwest, but coming over to work the Capitans from time to time, stopping off in Lincoln for a meal and a bed when it suited him. We rode off the mountain together, and were in Lincoln by late afternoon. He was a likable sort, and we got along well. I told him of the ranch and my family, inviting him to stop in whenever he pleased. We must have made been a sight riding into town, me on big Tom, and this "Bear" of a man wearing his beaded Blackfeet war shirt and dwarfing the mustang he rode.

We stabled our horses at the Wortley Hotel and got rooms, stowing our gear before meeting in the dining room. Our table was in a corner, and we both took chairs with our backs to a wall. The dinner hour was about to start and we just beat the rush. Amanda came over right away with a cheery greeting and took our orders after a short chat. She sure was friendly and seemed like a nice sort of girl, what little I knew of her. Each of us ate a juicy two inch thick steak with potatoes, carrots and green beans. The meat was cooked perfectly, seared a tad on the outside and almost red in the middle. Again the vegetables were fresh and tasty, the coffee hot and plentiful. When we finished eating, Amanda was right there to get our plates and promise to come back with more coffee. No sooner had she disappeared into the kitchen than she was back. With our coffee she brought us each a large piece of chocolate cake with sweet icing. Amanda said the cake was "on the house", that she'd baked it herself and hoped we would like it. Bear and I both stood up from our chairs and thanked her most kindly.

As we sat down and began eating the cake, Bear watched Amanda move around the dining room checking on the other customers.

He smiled slightly after swallowing his first bite and said "Mmm, now that girl can bake! If'n you ain't figured it out yet she's just as sweet as the icing on this cake, but she's sweet fer you."

I just looked at him and took another bite of cake, thinking on what he'd said. She was a nice girl, or rather woman not much younger than my little sister. Coming back to the area at the request of my brother I had not paid much attention to the treatment Amanda had given me each time I'd been to the hotel. It looked like I'd be around for a good while so perhaps I'd best pay her a little more attention when I have the chance. After all, Howell wasn't in town yet, and might not be for a few days more.

Bear and I sat at the table a long while after finishing the cake just watching folks and talking of times past. He'd come west from Missouri with his folks, headed for the California gold fields. His father was a merchant and planned to open a dry goods store once they found the right town. They made it as far as Tucson. His father was killed when the wagon fell on him as he changed a bad wheel. Bear and his mother went back to Missouri where they had family. A year later when he was sixteen, Bear headed west working on a wagon train. Seems he'd been bitten by the wide open country and had planned on returning ever since he and his mother went back east. He'd traveled north and got to know the mountains well, trapping some just to have money in his pocket when he went to a town. He'd missed the war but scouted for the army a few years afterward, getting into a few scrapes with the northern tribes. Yearning for the peace and quiet he'd known in the mountains but not wanting to stay away from people altogether, Bear ended up here. Plenty of mountains to trap and wander in and not but three or four days from a few towns. We adjourned to the porch for a spell just enjoying the cool evening air. Bear, eager for a real bed, headed for his room before I was quite ready for mine. Just sitting in my chair I was looking at the night, deep in thought.

Bear and I had sat through most of the supper crowd in the hotel restaurant and I sat there watching the last few customers step off the porch from my lonesome place in the darkness. I could hear the muffled clanging of pots and pans from the kitchen so they were still cleaning up inside. The ranch was really shaping up now and Bill was doing well. Howell was on his way and soon would be married to Maryellen, I imagine children would follow. The only one of us not settled down was me. Once just before riding into Sierrita I'd thought about putting down some roots but that did not work out. This is a nice area and if it were not for the trouble grumbling just beneath the surface it would be a peaceful place to settle down. Having all of my family here would be an added extra that made this a better place than all the others.

The lights inside went dim and there was a rustle of skirts at the hotel door. Amanda was just now leaving and I moved slightly to greet her, the movement startling her.

"I'm sorry Miss, didn't mean to surprise you. I was just

setting on the porch a while."

"Why that's all right." She replied softly "I should have used the window before coming outside. I'm glad it's you out here and not that Sam fellow."

"Somebody bothering you?" I asked.

"Not really, he's just too persistent. I wish he'd leave me alone, always asking to go on a picnic (pause) and he makes me uncomfortable."

"I'll walk you home if you'd like, Miss Amanda, just to be sure you make it to your door safely."

In the moonlight I could see she smiled just a little before saying "That would be very nice of you, but don't you think I should know your name first?"

"Seems like a good trade to me. My baptized name is, Michael, but my family and most everybody else has just been calling me 'Slim' for about as long as I can remember. If it's not being too familiar you could just use Slim."

Amanda tilted her head sort of funny for a few seconds and said "That would be fine, if you'll call me Amanda. It's only a short way, the Salazars rent me a small cabin behind their home."

Turning toward the porch steps I extended my arm to Amanda. She took it and we started off, quietly walking into a cool breeze from the mountain. Before long we reached her cabin and I asked if she lived there alone.

"Why yes, my parents were killed in a storm when we were coming west from Baltimore. Why do you ask?"

"Well, Amanda, if you're alone I'll stand outside for a few moments to be sure you get your lamp lit and there's no one hiding inside."

"That would be a comfort to me." She gently squeezed my left hand as she withdrew her arm from mine. "Thank you, Slim, goodnight." Amanda slipped inside and quietly closed the door behind her.

Turning my back to the wall of the house I looked northward to the bulk of Sierra Capitan. On the other side of those mountains my family was settled into their beds for the night and the twins were out in the desert keeping vigil as a favor to me. Amanda's light shown through the window onto the grass outside. After a few moments the light was out and I walked back toward the hotel. It was time I too went to sleep.

Awakening before first light I walked toward Tunstall's store. By the time that first ray of sunlight struck the treetops of the ridge south of town, I was sitting on a wooden bench, leaning against the store's front wall. It was peaceful just listening to the sounds of Lincoln coming alive, and watching as folks left their houses to tend livestock or get wood for breakfast's cook fire. Down the street past Murphy's store, the livery stable showed first movement, with the stable boy opening up to feed animals and muck out the stalls. Once the street became busier I left the cool shade of the porch, hungry for breakfast at the hotel.

CHAPTER SEVEN

Rounding a slight bend in the road I could see the fence in front of the hotel. As I neared the Salazar home, Amanda came into view, walking to work from her cabin. She saw me and almost immediately stopped short as if startled, then smiled embarrassingly, and continued toward the place where our paths crossed. We walked side by side to the hotel, with her explaining that when she first saw me she'd thought I was "...that Sam..." since he'd waited for her there a time or two. Just as we stepped through the hotel's front gate Amanda accepted an invitation to go on a picnic with me after the hotel's lunchtime and before dinner. She insisted on supplying the food, and I readily agreed to the arrangement.

After being sure the gate did not catch Amanda's skirt I straightened up and noticed a man sitting on the Wortley's porch. It was the same man I had tussled with in White Oaks. I remembered that his name also was Sam, and couldn't help but wonder if this was the same one that had been bothering Amanda. If he were then I was sure to find out soon enough.

As we climbed the porch steps Sam came to his feet and stood rigid, his jaw muscles tightening his mouth into a thin line. He glared angrily at me but remained silent. I'd opened the door for Amanda and when following her through touched the brim of my hat, smiling to Sam and said

"Howdy Sam, small world ain't it!"

Well if he had any nerves it surely looked like I'd struck one of them. But still, Sam remained silent. Amanda sort of giggled a tad so I must of struck a nerve with her too.

Since I'd been planning on breakfast anyway I headed for the dining room as Amanda disappeared into the kitchen. There was no one else here yet so I had my pick of the tables and took a seat against the back wall, looking across the dining room and out a window to the porch. After a minute or two the kitchen door came open a few inches and I could see the cook's face peering out. The door closed again and a few seconds later it opened and the cook walked over to my table, asking to sit a few minutes with me. I quickly invited him to join me and he sat down sort of nervously, introducing himself as Ralph. He and his wife had helped Amanda find work and a place to live when she'd first come to town with a few other families in wagons. Then he spoke of Sam.

"Slim, I always make it a point not to meddle in other folks business, but Amanda is special to me and my wife. If you're anything like your brother you're most likely a good man so I figure I just ought to tell you something."

He paused tentatively, looking around to make sure we were still alone.

"This Sam fella you spoke to outside, well he runs with a bad crowd. Don't know much about him, but some of his friends are sure to be killers when it'll do them good. I just thought you should know."

"Well Ralph, I surely appreciate your warning, but Sam and I know each other."

That surprised him, and I continued.

"Almost two weeks ago I was over in White Oaks with one of my nephews and Sam here thought he'd have some fun. We had a disagreement is all, I never seen him before then, and we ain't exactly friends."

He just looked at me for a moment and then Ralph spoke again.

"Amanda never said you already knew him or I'd not have bothered you."

"She doesn't know about it yet." I began. "There was never a need to tell her and I didn't know this fellow would turn out to be the same Sam that's been bothering her. Thank you though, for your concern."

Ralph excused himself and went back to work in the kitchen. He seemed likable enough, but definitely not your rough and tumble sort. Amanda came out shortly and began setting the tables for breakfast. By the time she worked her way to me, there were a few other folks sitting at a table across the room, and I could see a couple more coming through the gate. Amanda told me their normal breakfast was steak and eggs with coffee, but Ralph could make up something else if I wanted. I told her the regular was good enough for me and she checked at the other table before going back to the kitchen. It was a good steak and after finishing the meal I felt content.

After paying for breakfast I started to get up and Amanda told me that from the other table she could still see Sam out on the porch. I just nodded and told her I'd be back with a buggy for that picnic. Sam was still there all right, and he followed me off the porch into the yard and called for me to wait up. Before stopping I walked in an ark to the right so when I stopped, the hotel was no longer behind Sam. I'll give him one thing, Sam didn't waste any time this go around.

He just walked up close saying "That Amanda, she's my gal, and you ain't gonna pull no funny tricks on me this time."

Then he hit me in the stomach. I saw it coming

and just braced, letting him hit me. When it had no effect he looked stunned, and that's when I hit him square in the chest with a left, knocking the wind from his lungs. Looking him in the eye as he gasped for breath I said matter of factly,

"She ain't YOUR gal." And I caught him on the cheekbone with a right that spun him around and put him on the ground.

Backing up a few steps I just stood by while he pushed himself up to a kneeling position, still facing the other way. As Sam's breath returned, I caught a glimpse of Amanda standing on the porch with Ralph and a couple other folks. There were also two other gents standing just outside the gate who I recognized as being from the Murphy-Dolan crew.

After a few moments Sam had regained his wind and came to his feet while turning to face me. I told him to leave Miss Amanda alone since she was not interested in sharing his company. He just turned slowly to leave and even took a couple of steps before seeing his friends by the gate. Just that fast he made a grab for his pistol and spun around toward me. I'd been watching him pretty close and as he made his move I just slipped my pistol from it's holster thumbing the hammer at the same time. Sam had turned a mite faster than he could bring his gun around and as his body faced me I fired once, then a second time as he continued bringing up his pistol. Both bullets made their mark in his chest, the second one stopping him cold. Turning to his friends at the gate I saw one of them start to reach but the other grabbed him and said something, saving the man's life.

Speaking out I asked, "You boys want to draw any cards in this game?"

"No sir." Said the second man as he took a hand from his partner's shoulder. "I seen you in Arizona Territory a few years back didn't I? You'd be Sierrita Slim."

"I wore a badge in Sierrita. This fight look fair to you fellas?"

"Shore did, Sam never was much good at pickin' who to fight with."

I spoke to them again saying, "You boys get a wagon and haul him off will you, these good people are trying to eat breakfast."

Reloading my pistol as the two men walked off together, I holstered up and walked back to the porch. As I neared the steps a few of the folks turned and walked inside, Amanda and Ralph remained. Ralph figured I'd given Sam every chance and told me so before going back inside to work. Amanda remained just long enough to speak with me a short time.

"I didn't mean to cause this." She said. "I'm sorry I got you involved."

"You didn't cause anything." I replied. "Sam already started one fight with me, this was bound to happen again with us both being in the same town. He never would have gone for his gun except he tried to show off for his two friends."

She nodded slowly and reached for my left hand, clasping it between both of hers.

"I'm glad you're all right. Will you still come around for me later?"

"Of course, I'm still mighty curious to see if your lunch is as good as that cake!"

Amanda smiled and walked into the dining room, getting back to her work. More people showed up looking for a good breakfast, walking past Sam's body lying in the grass, still wet with morning dew. Before too long those fellas came back to pick up Sam's body. Bob Ollinger, the town marshal came with them. After they hauled Sam off, Ollinger came onto the porch and spoke with me about the shooting. There was no trouble, and he seemed more interested in getting a look at me than in the shooting, talking only briefly of his duty to keep the peace in town. Bob, I recall, had a reputation with his pistols back in Indian Country before coming to the Pecos Valley to join his brother Wallace who's ranch is near Seven Rivers. Another gunman, Dutch Charlie Kruling had come from Oklahoma with Bob.

With Bob's brother having a ranch near Dolan's, that surely made the connection between Murphy's "House" and the local law. I wasn't sure where that put my brother and I in their minds, what with Bill doing work for Chisum and the army sometimes. Me killing Sam couldn't help matters any, but at least our argument wasn't over anything important to those rustlers. It's fortunate they had not figured out who it was that had shot those two men in the rocks east of

town and the other one at the branding fire to the
south.

The rest of the morning went by pretty quickly.
Walking to the livery I spoke with the blacksmith and
paid up front to rent a buggy for the afternoon. At
Tunstall's I bought a heavy wool blanket for the picnic,
figuring with the nights getting colder and all the folks
at the ranch it would be useful later. Then I went back
to the hotel to clean my pistol before having a bath and
shave. After brushing my pants and coat I finished
dressing, wearing a clean shirt I'd brought along. The
lunch crowd was thinning so I headed back to the livery
where the buggy was ready and waiting for me. On the
way back to the hotel for Amanda I stopped again at
Tunstall's store. I had left the blanket I'd bought, not
feeling like carrying it around town on foot. There
were a few men on the steps of Murphy's store
watching me drive past, but they didn't seem to want
any trouble.

After tying the buggy to the fence near the hotel's
gate I started walking toward the porch where I'd wait,
not wanting to bother Amanda while she was working.
Timing was perfect and before I could climb the steps
Amanda came through the door with her arm through
the handle of a covered wicker basket. With her other
arm she took mine and I turned toward the buggy and a
short drive to a shaded spot I'd seen near the river. We
drove west out of town before turning north from the
main road on a wagon trail that crossed the Rio Bonito.
Near the river there's a grassy meadow with a few large
oak trees for shade. After driving in the picket pin we
walked closer to the water before spreading the blanket.
Sitting for a few moments we just watched the water
and listened to the chuckles it made jumping over some

rocks near the bank. It's amazing how peaceful the world seems when there's a stream running nearby and you're in no hurry to move on. Just a few yards away the ground was hard as a brick, but here by the water the grass grows thick and juicy, covering the dirt with a soft cool cushion.

Not really knowing what to say I just sat there until Amanda flipped up the lid to the basket and started pulling out food. First out were a few biscuits, not the hard ones like I'm used to, but soft and fresh like for a Thanksgiving dinner. I guess working in a restaurant had it's advantages, because next out of the basket were celery stalks and cucumber slices! I hadn't seen them since El Paso! Last but certainly not least was the fried chicken, plump and crispy!

At first we just talked back and forth about the food but as the eating slowed, our conversation drifted to my family. I felt comfortable talking with her and so told Amanda more about my family and myself than I had before. She seemed to get quiet for a short time and said how she missed having a family around her. Thinking how she was not much younger than my sister I mentioned that perhaps sometime I could bring her out to the ranch. She brightened up at the idea. That made me feel good but at the same time I wondered what it was I had in mind.

Explaining about the concern Bill has for the safety of his family and that I had the same concern, it was comforting to hear from Amanda that she understood and was also a little worried about what it seemed was developing in the valley. Telling Amanda the main concern I had was for my family's well being, I added that I would visit her whenever my other responsibilities permitted. She looked away for a moment with a saddened look about her. Smiling, I spoke up saying her name.

She looked at me hesitantly before I told her "I like your company, and if it won't be an imposition I'll come visit as often as I can."

Brightening up she said softly and with a smile, "No imposition at all Slim, I'd like that. I enjoy your company too."

We both sat quietly for a few minutes, then Amanda started gathering up her things so we could go back to town. She still had to work the dinner hour, and it had been at least a couple of hours since we left the hotel. Leaving Amanda at the blanket I went over to the buggy, pulled the pin and led the horse over to Amanda. With each of us taking an end we folded the blanket before I put everything in the back and helped Amanda up to the seat.

It was just a few yards out of the meadow and when we were about a fifty yards from the road into Lincoln the stage rolled by with the horses at a fast trot. There was a tall, lean man wearing city clothes up on top with the driver. Wondering if it might be Howell I became anxious to get back to town. Once we turned onto the main road I shook out the reigns, letting the horse have his head. Figuring we were headed home he stepped up to a slow canter, most likely in a hurry to be free of his harness. As we neared the edge of town the road curved to the left. We could see past Murphy's store and on up to Tunstall's before the road curved out of our view. The stage had pulled up in front of Tunstall's store, the tall one was standing beside it stretching the stiffness from his muscles. I recognized that stretch, and it was surely my future brother-in-law.

The two men that had stood by the hotel gate when I shot Sam were a few yards away from Howell when the driver got the luggage untied from the roof and tossed two bags down to him. The men walked right up to Howell and started to crowd him a mite, the one who had recognized me was letting the other one do the talking. Amanda expressed concern for Howell, what with these two roughnecks looking like they were trying to cause some trouble. Slowing to a walk, I stopped the buggy twenty yards from the stage. Howell was facing partly in the other direction and didn't notice us. Once more Amanda asked if I shouldn't get down and announce myself to avoid trouble.

"Those men don't know Howell, he's often misjudged." I said quietly with a smile. "If they want to start something with him they'll get their due. I'll jump in if he needs a hand."

He was pushing Howell all right, and Howell was as calm as if he were sitting at his own supper table. It was easy to see he was trying to avoid trouble, but unfortunately for them it looked like the others thought they had him spooked. I know Howell doesn't like trouble like this, but he doesn't spook either. They both moved very close to Howell reaching out to each grab an arm. Seemed like they had it in mind to throw him in the water trough. The one that had started to draw on me earlier grabbed Howell's left wrist first.

Howell surprised him with a fast solid right to the jaw, knocking him off the boardwalk into the dirt near the horses. As Howell struck, the second man moved in but Howell had him pegged. Drawing his right arm backward from the jaw of the first man he threw his weight into the second man, hitting him square in the face with his elbow. Following through with the elbow Howell watched the man fall to the ground, out cold, with blood flowing freely from his nose. Gathering himself off the ground the first man fumbled to unlash his pistol when Howell turned back toward him, pulling a Colt Navy conversion from his waistband. The slower man knew he was beaten and stopped, slowly opening his hands, waiting to see what Howell would do with the pistol he had so quickly produced.

"I'll choose what drink washes the dust from my throat, friend." Quipped Howell, "You boys did this to yourselves." He placed the pistol back in his pants before continuing. "See to your friend, it looks like he could use some help."

Watching as one of his attackers helped the other away, Howell turned abruptly and walked toward our buggy straightening his vest with a smile. He'd seen us pull up after all. I reckon there's no moss growing on his boots.

CHAPTER EIGHT

As Howell neared the buggy I hopped to the ground. He tipped his hat toward Amanda first, then turned to me.

"Hey Slim! Seems like it's been a spell." Taking my hand in a strong grip we greeted each other. I shook his in both my hands, he's like another brother to me.

"It has, good to see you again. My sister's gonna be happy you made it alright." I said.

"Did you arrange my greeting party or has Lincoln become a different sort of town?"

"It's still a good place, and Bill is doing well. But there are some folks on the prod around here, there may be something in the wind. Those two that jumped you watched me kill a friend of theirs this morning, he didn't give me a choice." I informed him.

"Watched you? Howell queried. "Seems like their sort would try to step in."

"The one that moved on you first started to but he was a tad slow." I hesitated a moment. "The one with the broken nose recognized me and stopped him. I'll fill you in later, but for now meet a friend of mine."

After officially introducing him to Amanda we put Howell's luggage on the buggy. Howell sat next to his bags facing rearward and dangling his legs over the edge. I took Amanda back to the Wortley so she could work the dinner hour. Leaving Howell to get a room and clean up I drove the buggy back to the livery stable to return it. Inside I found Bear. Having just finished tying his packs he was preparing to mount up and leave town. I thought it was odd, his leaving in mid-afternoon but he planned on sleeping somewhere on Sierra Capitan tonight and looking for fresh bear sign first thing in the morning. Turns out he'd been in the livery packing up when the stage came in. Seeing me close behind he'd watched to see if Howell had come in on the stage. He saw what happened and told me to ride careful a while. Those two fellas that jumped Howell had been talking when they walked past the stable on the way to "the House". They were not happy with the way things turned out, and had noticed our warm greeting. Needless to say they didn't care for me too much either.

Wishing him a good hunt I watched Bear ride off to the west toward the edge of town. After returning the buggy I went out behind the stable to the corrals, walking to the far side and leaning on the top rail I watched the horses and thought things over a while. It surely would be nice if no trouble came of this day's excitement, but I could not believe we'd seen the end of it. Walking around the livery I headed back to the hotel.

Sitting on the front porch was Howell, feet up on the railing and a contented expression on his face. It had been a long journey to go back east, clean up all the loose ends with his ship and return to start a new life. My sister was a part of this new life, and though he was anxious to see Maryellen again he was glad just to be a few hours ride from her for a change.

Tomorrow would see us back at the ranch. I took my place in a chair near Howell. We relaxed, bringing each other up to date on things of interest and plans for the future. When folks began showing up for dinner we went inside and sat at the table that had become my usual place to set.

The meal was delicious and Amanda seemed in especially bright spirits. Howell and I took our time with the food and eventually adjourned to the porch. After his long trip Howell was ready for sleep and as soon as his food settled went to his room. Wanting to walk Amanda home after the kitchen closed but not wishing to sit still until then I walked through town, lingering near the stone torreon. There are several of these towers along the Rio Bonito and Rio Ruidoso, built as a safe place for the settlers to retreat to under threat of attack. I went inside and climbed up on top where I sat and enjoyed the clear star-lit sky for a few minutes. It was getting nigh onto time for Amanda to finish up so I climbed down and headed back to my seat on the hotel porch.

There wasn't much business in the dining room tonight, matter of fact the whole town seemed unusually calm. Before long Amanda came outside for a breath of fresh air and visited a few minutes with me. Turns out they were going to close early tonight since it was so quiet. I told her that suited me fine since I wanted to walk her home, and also try to get to bed before it got too late. Amanda went inside and finished her work quickly, leaving the last few chores for Ralph as usual.

Amanda took my arm as we stepped from the porch. It was early November now, and a cold chill was in the air. Just through the gate Amanda squeezed my arm closer against her and commented on the cool night. I agreed winter was coming on, and the nights would be colder yet. Still was the night, for not a sound was to be heard anywhere except our footfalls as we rounded the Salazar's home and Amanda's house came into view. Once at the door I reminded Amanda that Howell and I would be riding back to the ranch in the morning, but that I'd see her again before too long. Still holding my left arm she looked up, lifting her other hand to touch my mustache. Then without saying a word Amanda stood on her toes and lightly kissed my cheek before disappearing through her open door, closing it quietly behind her. Once her lantern was lit I walked back to the hotel and went to sleep, for tomorrow would be an early day.

The first light of the day saw Howell and I a couple miles from town headed for the ranch. We'd left

Lincoln going west, planning to cross Sierra Capitan at the pass. It would be the most obvious place for us to go, but it was also the fastest way back home. In the center of the pass, tracks of two horses that had been traveling north broke off to the west heading onto the southern face of West Mountain. It was rocky, rough terrain there and whoever it was would have a difficult time just staying on the game trails.

After watering at Gum Spring we anxiously rode to the ranch, coming in sight of it from almost due east early in the afternoon. The skies off to the west were dark and full of warning. It seemed like bad weather was moving in on the ranch. Even in the winter, weather was mostly clear, but when storms came through they really cut loose. Nearing the ranch Howell noticed Bill's improvements right away, but there was no activity outside. Still a couple hundred yards out we circled the barn to get a clear view of the houses. Tied in front of the main house were half a dozen horses.

We rode in easy, until I recognized two of them as Bear's, two belonged to Hank and Frank, the others were tied to Bear's pack horse and had dead men lashed across the saddles. All of the family came out to meet us, Maryellen moving to Howell's side as we dismounted. Frank stood in the doorway. As serious faces greeted Howell I walked around to where I could see the dead men. They were the same two who had jumped Howell as he arrived in Lincoln. Bill and I shook hands, then headed inside, the others followed us.

Bear was sitting at the table with a plate of food half empty in front of him, a grin found it's way to his face as he stood and stepped from the table. He'd already told Bill and the family most of what had happened, so Luke and Matt headed outside to tend to the animals. Earlier this morning Bear had his horse tethered as he checked for animal signs near Jacob Spring on foot. Hearing horses coming he remained hidden. These two men had ridden up to the spring for a breather and while watering their horses spoke of plans to ambush Howell and I as we rode toward the ranch. Seems they figured we'd stop at Gum Spring and they'd hit us from a ridge as we rode past Encinoso Canyon.

Letting the talk continue so he had more time to think on the situation, Bear decided what to do about the same time as those two gathered up their horses to mount. After positioning himself from a good angle to catch them in the open, Bear stepped out with the big .50 in his hand. Moving without sound he was about fifteen yards from them when he spoke out.

"Stand still boys, while I read to you a bit."

Each of them had saddle in one hand with hair and reigns in the other, one foot reaching for a stirrup. They didn't know just what was happening, but they did realize they were in a bad way. As told to, they let both feet go to the ground but kept their hands on the horses. Listening quietly they were told Bear intended to keep them under watch for a couple hours to give Howell and I time to make it out well past their ambush point then let them go back to Lincoln. All went well at first while Bear had them one at a time tie their horse and find a comfortable place to take a nap for a while. The second man to tie his horse was the first to try and take Bear. As he turned from the horse he drew his pistol, catching a .50 caliber Sharps bullet in the chest. The other, not seeing any gun except for the single shot big bore moved for his pistol as well. He was slowed some by his seated position and Bear had more than enough time to pull a Merwin Hulbert .44 pistol from underneath his war shirt. They fired at about the same time. In his hurry the outlaw's bullet only found some dirt near Bear's feet, but the big man's pistol spoke twice finding it's mark both times.

Not having any reason to wait around the spring and not wishing to take a chance on missing me as Howell and I made our way off of the mountain, Bear decided to head for the ranch. He was lashing the second man onto his saddle when the twins rode up. They'd been about a mile west and riding for the spring when they heard the shots. Hank and Frank were no pilgrims and they came in quickly at first to close some ground and get to better cover. Once nearing the spring they moved much more carefully and at the ready.

With the noises he was making with his chore Bear didn't hear the twins ride up until he just had time to stand clear of the horses and pick up his rifle before he was facing Hank and Frank. The twins had separated a few yards, making it difficult for Bear to get them both if it came to shooting. From the way I'd spoken of them, Bear knew right away who it was he was facing and talked up first.

"You two must be the brothers Slim told me of, been with him on and off since the war."

"That would be us." Frank said, "Who are you, and what happened here?"

Well it was easy going from there, and with all he knew about the situation the twins figured I must trust him so they would too. The group gathered up everything and after getting Bear's horses rode for the ranch. They'd been there about an hour when Howell and I rode in.

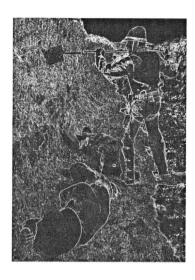

CHAPTER NINE

After we talked over the situation a while, the twins and I along with Bear, took the two bodies and rode to the northeast a few miles till we crossed Carrizo Creek. It was in a caved in section of a dirt bank where we laid them under the overhang before collapsing more of the bank over top of them. On the way back to the ranch we stopped to water in the creek, taking time to wash dried blood from the saddles. Once back home Luke stowed the dead men's gear and turned their horses out into the corral. I'd be taking them back to Lincoln in a day or two, it wouldn't do to keep quiet again and have Murphy's people get suspicious. I'd been lucky with the way things had turned out after that branding fire, and again with the "ambush" east of town. No need to push our luck any further, especially when these two came after us for a reason that is known to folks and has nothing to do with the other problems brewing in Lincoln.

We spent that evening and the next day keeping busy with normal chores about the ranch. Lunchtime called for a long break from work so we could do some more catching up on news from back east. Howell knew we'd be interested so he'd taken a good tally of who was doing what before heading west. The plans for his freight business were incomplete, but Howell was leaning toward finding a building in Lincoln that could serve as office, stable and home. That would mean he and Maryellen would have to move into town and they had not yet discussed it in private. Whatever they decided would be fine with the rest of us and we'd help in any way we could.

Just after breakfast of the following day, Luke, Bear and I left for Lincoln with horses and gear from the dead men. Matt had been to Lincoln with me before so I figured on squaring things with Luke. Except for the time when Bear or I rode out front a ways, the three of us rode abreast of each other talking quietly about anything that came to mind. It made the ride go quickly and we dismounted in front of the sheriff's office by mid afternoon. Bob Ollinger had just returned from a late lunch at the Wortley and recognized the extra horses right away.

After telling him of the trouble Howell had when he first got into town a few nights ago we told him of the ambush plans of the two men and the fate they had met. Ollinger didn't seem surprised by the ambush which made me wonder if perhaps he knew of the plans ahead of time. He did show sign of discontent with the manner in which Bear had thrown sand in with the grease, thwarting the ambush. Shaking his head slowly the sheriff commented that although we were probably telling the truth, Mr. Murphy more than likely wouldn't like hearing of the death of his men. I told Ollinger to be sure and tell Murphy that this whole matter had nothing to do with anyone beside these two men, Howell and me. They didn't like me since the trouble I'd had with Sam over a woman, and they had started their own trouble with Howell. Coming after us only made things worse for themselves. If they'd not started trouble with us they'd more than likely still be setting on the porch at Murphy's store.

After telling us he didn't think there would be any further trouble over this, the sheriff headed off to deliver horses and gear to Murphy. The three of us rode over to the hotel. Luke and I would spend the night in town so we signed for rooms. Bear wanted to head back into the mountains right away so he waited outside with all the horses. Once we'd registered, Luke and I took our horses out to the hotel's barn and tended to them. We talked a mite with Bear, and once we were finished with the horses Bear rode off to once again start his hunting.

Luke and I walked past the torreon to Tunstall's store where we bought some licorice whips and sat on the porch, just enjoying the inactivity. Minutes passed and it was getting on toward suppertime. There was almost no movement on the street, until two well dressed men came out of Murphy's store, mounted horses that had been tied out front, and rode up the street in our direction. One of them was much larger than the other, and the smaller man rode just slightly behind the other as if following his lead. It seemed to me as if I had attracted their attention somehow so I told Luke to just sit tight. Once closer they turned toward us and drew reign, stopping directly in front of me. Luke and I just sat there slouched on the porch bench with our legs stretched out across the boardwalk, chewing on licorice.

The bigger man looked at me a moment before speaking up, still setting his horse.

"I'm L.G. Murphy, owner of the 'house' down the street, this here's my partner, JJ Dolan. Would you be this 'Slim' fella my boys keep having trouble with?"

"Not exactly." I said, still stretched out, "I'm the fella your boys keep pickin' fights with, and I surely wish they'd leave me be."

"Well I'm glad to hear that, I thought you might be trying to start something." He replied.

Responding I said, "Me, why I'm just visiting my family after a couple years away."

"Sounds like you'll be moving on then?" He queried. "Be sure and stop by my store sometime before you leave, might have something for you."

"Well sir, mostly I stop at the Wortley, and your place is another quarter mile past here to walk to. But you never know, I'll think on it."

"You do that." Murphy spit. "Maybe I can make you an offer that'll keep you around a while."

"Now I doubt that, I've had all the excitement I can stand already. Anyways, I'm thinking on settling down ` with my brother." I said easily.

"We'll be glad to have your business." He finished. "I'll make sure my boys don't pick any trouble with you, long as you don't start nothing."

Murphy whirled his horse around and trotted off the way he'd come, Dolan on his heels. Looking over at Luke, he still sat there, an unfinished piece of licorice in his hand. I slapped him on the knee and stood up, suggesting we hike back to the hotel for dinner.

"Uncle, seems to me they rode up here special just to talk to you. Why?" Queried Luke.

Hesitating a few moments I responded. "Murphy's got a good thing going with his store, Chisum's stock, and the local law on his side. Six of his men have been killed lately, three of them were involved with me somehow that he knows of. One of them died in a stand up Gunfight. I have a reputation putting me on the side of the law but not his kind of law. He just wanted to see what I look like and try to figure if I'm a fly in his ointment."

We walked on a bit and I could tell Luke was deep in thought. Not even thinking about it he put his hand to his hip, checking the position of his holstered colt.

"Luke." I said, "The best thing for us to do is go about our business and pay all those fellers no mind."

A little excited, but with a seriousness about him, Luke returned, "But Uncle, if something happens I want to help."

"You do a man's work, Luke, and if they start trouble I'll be glad to have you by my side. Wouldn't have it any other way. I know you're anxious to help protect the family, but if any of them think you're anxious for trouble they may bring it on when it's not necessary just to get at me. We'll just mind our own affairs and keep alert for signs of trouble so we're ready if need be. Now let's have a good steak and relax, life's too short to worry for nothing."

"Yes sir, I am fairly hungry."

The full moon was up early this evening and the chill had been coming on since the sun went behind some clouds above the horizon. We walked up the steps into the hotel's restaurant amidst the clamor of plates and silverware. About half of the tables were full, but we were still able to take a table against the back wall. Amanda spotted us right off as she came out of the kitchen with an armload of plates. As soon as she dropped the food off at another table, Amanda came toward us, straightening her blouse and a wisp of hair that had fallen across her face as she came.

Speaking to Luke as she approached, Amanda began her greeting, "Well you're a good bit taller than Matt and some older too. You must be Luke!"

"Yes ma'am." Responded Luke, pushing back his chair and coming to his feet. Hat in his hand but still a bit nervous.
"Thought I'd bring him along so you could meet the

family one at a time!"

I spoke up, following Luke's lead, I too came to my feet, doffing my hat. "Good evening, Amanda. It's good to see you again."

"You men ought to remember where you are and sit down before you gather too much attention with your politeness! What'll it be, supper?"

"Supper, desert, and a walk to your door after that if you'd like." I said.

Amanda simply replied "I would." And smiled happily as she spun around and headed for the kitchen.

After Luke and I finished off our over-stuffed plates we each had a large slice of apple pie to contend with. Since it wasn't a full dining room there was no need for us to clear the table too soon. We ate slowly, savoring the meal, and talking about whatever came to mind. Amanda stopped by to visit for a few moments when she could. I really enjoyed talking with Luke, he had many plans for his future to mull over and we had a good time talking without the rest of the family around.

Before too long it was time to walk Amanda home, so Luke excused himself and went to his room for the night. With darkness, the night had turned cold so Amanda and I stood in the dining room talking for several minutes before going outside for the walk to her house. She'd heard about the gear we'd brought into town. The whole thing didn't surprise her, knowing what kind of men they were and having seen the incident with Howell she figured they'd try to get even somehow. Once outside it was surprising how black the night was. Normally, even without a moon there was plenty of light from just the stars. The clouds near the horizon earlier had taken over the sky, blocking out the starlight. We walked briskly the short distance to Amanda's house and once she was inside with a light lit I didn't linger in the cold. These clouds could mean bad weather so Luke and I had best leave early if we could. I checked the horses and our gear before going to sleep.

Waking in darkness I stepped to the window, sliding it open to check outside. Shielding my lamp from the wind I could see the snow was just beginning to fall. We'd best be on our way quickly if we wanted to make it back to the ranch before next week.

Tapping lightly on Luke's door so's not to wake anyone else, I woke him easily. It took only a few minutes for me to get dressed and gather my things. When opening the door to my room I found Luke, ready to ride and anxious to hit the trail. Figuring on leaving early regardless of the weather I'd paid our bill the night before so we slipped quietly outside and went to the barn. After giving our horses a portion of grain from the bin we prepared and saddled them as they fed. Needing heat the grain would provide and knowing we were about to ride, my Tom and Luke's bay horse ate hungrily. We warmed the steel bits in our hands before putting them into the mouths of our horses, taking care as we slipped the bridles over their ears.

Half an hour later we were well on our way. With the storm coming from the northwest we figured on riding around West Mountain past Jacob Spring. This would hopefully keep us somewhat protected from the brunt of the wind until we rounded the mountain and headed across mostly open country for the ranch. The rest of our ride would be the shortest leg and we'd be riding across the wind and snow rather than into it.

Somewhere above the storm was a bright, starlit sky shining down on top of the storm. A hazy sort of opaque light shone evenly through the clouds, making the storm itself seem to give off enough light to guide us. We loped up the roadway, wanting to make good time where we could. Knowing that once off the road we'd be forced to a walk, unable to see what lay beneath the snow and not wanting our horses to miss-step. It seemed like just a few minutes and we were off the road and had crossed the Rio Bonito. A chill was just beginning to work it's way through my outer layer of clothing. Glancing at Luke I could tell it was the same with him. We pushed along steadily until we got to our usual watering spot, Jacob spring. It was iced over a bit but the horses had an easy chore breaking through with their hooves to get at the water. It was full light now and the storm didn't seem to be as bad as it might, even looked like it might be clearing over toward the ranch. Luke mentioned a small cave nearby so I'd know about it if I ever needed shelter.

Before long we crossed the icy creek and were riding into the ranch yard. There were several inches of snow on the ground and except for a few of them the horses were all under shelter. Luke and I put up our tack, letting the horses loose in the corral. It always seems funny to me that the first thing a horse will do when you let him loose is roll around on the ground to scratch his back and rough up the hair matted down by the saddle. The snow made no difference, both of them rolled right after we let them go, getting wet and muddy from the ground that had been trampled by the other horses during the night.

As Luke and I walked toward the main house, Bill and Hank stepped outside waiting for us on the porch. They were relieved there had been no more trouble in town over the incident and the four of us joined everyone else inside. Sarah and Maryellen were preparing a big meal, the rest were just sitting around doing small chores or simply relaxing in the heat from the stove. Matt stopped the bridle repair he was doing long enough to say hello, he seemed disappointed somewhat that our trip to town had been a quiet one. Frank, who was napping on the floor, opened his eyes, took an elbow to say hello and hear what little news there was. He'd have to wait until we pealed off our outer clothing and had a hot cup of coffee in our hands before we'd talk though. We'd had a cold ride and were anxious to get the blood flowing quickly. Me? I was delighted nothing else had happened while Luke and I were in town. The rest of the family along with Hank and Frank had just stayed close to home, waiting to see if anyone would come looking for their missing friends. When it looked like a storm might be brewing the night before, they secured tools and supplies that might blow away in a strong wind, and stacked firewood on the porches. When they awoke this morning the storm was already upon them and a few inches of snow covered everything.

Once again it was good to be back at the home ranch. With the weather it looked as if we'd have at least a couple of days rest before doing much work. I didn't mind though, and I don't think anyone else did either.

CHAPTER TEN

The snow stopped falling early in the afternoon and sunshine broke through the clouds just before the sun fell behind Carrizo mountain on it's daily journey to the other side of the world. With the brief sunlight came promise of improved weather for tomorrow and our evening was a lazy one with early bedtimes for us all. Bill and I were the last to bed down, enjoying a few minutes quiet conversation on the porch before I walked to the other house and my temporary bed.

In typical fashion for the territory, sunlight, bright and warm announced the new day. When the stock had been checked and breakfast finished, spots of brown dirt were already showing through the snow all across the desert. As bad as the weather could get in this part of the country it's amazing how quickly it could change back to sunny and hot. We spent the afternoon planning for the next couple of weeks and Howell's new purchase.

He'd paid earnest money on a couple of wagons that awaited him in Albuquerque and wanted to pick them up before Thanksgiving, just a few weeks away. There was also the building in Lincoln that he'd expressed interest in renting and needed to make final arrangements for. The only other family business needing to be done was finishing off the horses for John Chisum.

Completing our plans as the sun finished melting most of the snow, we knew what preparations had to be made the next day. Yes sir, no matter how you looked at it, the things we'd do from now to Thanksgiving would start a new era for our family. After a relaxed and filling supper we let the rest of the family know what we'd all be doing in the near future.

Tomorrow would be spent preparing for the trip to Albuquerque and Howell's wagons. That would let the sun dry the earth for one more day before we traveled. Luke and I would ride into Lincoln along with Howell, Hank and Frank. After the other three left on the stage, Luke and I would return with all the horses. Matt was disappointed that he would miss his turn at going to town but being in the middle of a week long chore he understood. Besides, after two more weeks passed I would return to Lincoln with saddle horses for Howell and the twins. Matt would accompany me then.

This put into motion the last stages of preparation for the business that would support Howell and Maryellen when they were married come spring time. We were all excited for them. Always enjoying surprises I went and put another iron into the fire that threw sparks everywhere and got everybody all worked up even more. I'd been thinking a lot about the family and how I've been roaming the countryside since the war, with no real plans for myself. The realization came to me that what I'm lacking is a family of my own.

While talking with my brother on the porch the night before, Bill insisted that I throw in with him and join the horse business. We'd been close as youngsters and both wanted that kinship again. My wandering days might soon be over, depending on the wife I'd chosen. While in Lincoln this trip I would talk to Amanda and invite her out to the ranch for Thanksgiving. That way she could meet the entire family, seeing how we live and make our living.

Everyone was all excited now, including me and with all the talk, bed time was very late in coming. What with all the smiles and giddiness you'd of thought the arrangements were made already and the date was set. All I'd really done was make sure I had a way to support a wife and family if Amanda was agreeable! Eventually everyone got tired and meandered off to their beds, even the women!

Once again the new day began with sudden brilliant sunlight from the east. With moisture from the melted snow still in the air there was a heavy, sparkling dew on everything. It dripped from the roofs and colored the ground a dark, damp brown as if there had been a light rain during the night. Brisk would describe the temperature, below 40 degrees and just a hint of movement in the air. I could see the moisture in my breath as I stepped from the porch and walked toward the corrals where Luke and Matt were already at work checking the stock. Taking the pitchfork from Matt I helped Luke toss hay into the corral. Matt started pumping water that would fill the trough and run down the spillway to the corral where the horses could drink. The snow hadn't done any damage and since melting, it's moisture is in the ground where it would do us some good. Before long the temperature would be up in the 70's or even higher, the hot sun drying trails to town for tomorrow's ride. We finished the yard chores about the same time as Maryellen walked outside and headed for the main house. We met her on the way and together went inside for our meal.

After breakfast everyone tended to their chores. I helped Bill check the horses he's been working and we discussed different ways to get what we wanted out of them. We still think alike in many ways and I was anxious to make more of a contribution to the ranch. Not to say I wasn't working the stock with him, but I needed to always keep the trouble brewing in the territory to mind and watch for situations that might affect the family.

Once Howell and the twins had gone for the wagons the rest of us would be working around the ranch. But for a time, plans were that I would be gone with one of the boys. The first trip out, getting Howell to the stage would be a short trip for Luke and me, leaving Bill home with just Matt for only one overnight. Later, when Matt and I went to Lincoln with saddle horses for the returning men, we'd be waiting in town for maybe a few days depending on how quickly Howell and the others could make it back. That would leave Bill with the elder Luke to help in case of trouble. There were still problems once in a while on outlying ranches and though the territory was mostly peaceful to those not involved in local politics, we needed to be alert most all of the time just to be on the safe side.

The day would pass quickly at the ranch with everyone in a hurry to finish chores and ready equipment for the next day's adventure. About mid-morning Frank and I mounted up and headed toward Jacob Spring as if we were riding to Lincoln. Seeing no sign, wc mixed our tracks with those of animals watering at the spring and cut back to the east, staying in the shadow of the Sleeping Maiden as we worked our way around the ranch. Staying about four or five miles out, we were watchful for any sign of movement that didn't belong. Keeping up a pretty good pace we broke for a cold meal just after noontime in the breaks north of the ranch about mid way between Reventon Draw and Carrizo Creek.

Coming across a nice spot just below the peak of a ridge line we sat back on a rocky ledge above the small grassy bowl our horses grazed in. Hidden from all directions except the one we'd come from we were protected from the chill in the breeze and had the sun to bake us into a lull. The horses were content to eat grass and drink from the runoff of a slow seep dripping from the base of our ledge, not bothered by their hobbles in the least. We could just see our ranch in the distance, too far away to make out any activity. It was a pretty little picnic spot and we could have stayed there all day, sheltered from the wind, eating sandwiches we'd packed and basking in the high desert sun.

Enjoying the relaxation, I was taking my time with lunch. Frank finished first and was just settling back for a few moments nap when he noticed some movement on a ridge about two miles closer to the ranch than us. Two riders moving slowly. They were coming from the west and on the near side of a small rise, hidden from the ranch but open to our watching eyes. Could be they were headed for Roswell from the country north of White Oaks. At least that's what we figured until they dismounted and climbed up to the top of the rise. Frank was already lying down, his movement more difficult to see from a distance such as this. I remained in my position as Frank crept off of the ledge and down to the horses for my telescope. We needed to see what those men were up to.

Shielding the glass from reflection that might give us away, I could see they'd tied their horses to a greasewood and moved up to the hilltop where they could lay flat while watching the ranch. It looked like one of them had a telescope of his own. From our position we could see the area's terrain like a maze, and chose a path through the breaks that would lead us around to them from the west. We could move up on them from the same direction they'd come, one they'd be less likely to watch.

Back in the war, we'd sometimes set up an attack by watching our targets ahead of time when we had the chance. On the frontier, renegades often sent scouts out to set up patterns of movement on the ranches they would raid. This helped them figure out when fighters would be separated from each other or in a place that would be more difficult to defend. If that's what these men were doing, we'd best be careful.

The ridge Frank and I were on was the divider between Carrizo Creek and Reventon Draw. The terrain sloped off toward the ranch from here in a series of small ridges and draws we call breaks. After mounting up we rode out of the bowl we'd hobbled the horses in and circled around to the west, keeping to low ground and a fast lope. With the round-a-bout path we took, in about 30 minutes we'd closed half the distance and stopped to check our spies. I climbed up one of the ridges we were using as cover and lay in the shade of a small bush. The men were still there, watching our ranch.

We climbed back into the saddle and headed out once again. This time we moved at a walk so as not to make any noise that could alert the men or their horses. We were still almost a mile away from them but sound carries a long way in open country. A hoof turning a rock or a winded horse wanting to 'blow' could betray our presence, so careful we rode. Tying the horses to a greasewood with just one small ridge separating us from the men, we crept slowly up the ridge into a small cholla patch for concealment. The men were collecting their gear and preparing to ride so we stayed put and watched.

They were traveling light without any packs or extra blankets and rode back the way they came, seemingly without a care in the world. We waited till they were out of sight around a bend in the draw before leaving our position. Frank and I decided to stay with the horses a bit before taking a look at any sign the men left behind. It was plain to see they had ridden out here for the sole purpose to watch the ranch. We needed to know as much as we could about these men.

Frank and I walked toward the trail keeping to hard ground so as not to leave any sign of our own. Turns out the trail they used was exactly that, a trail leading up to their lookout and going no further. Four sets of tracks all made today. These two riders must have been the relief for another pair who stood watch in the morning. That makes it a group of at least four, probably camped in the tree line off to the west a few more miles. We mounted and after riding another half mile to the north we headed west slowly, wanting to come up to the trees just before dark.

As the sun started dropping behind the mountains to the west, the breeze suddenly went quiet. Knowing we were maybe headed for trouble, the stillness was almost eerie. Not wanting to chance a reflection giving away our position we waited until the sun was entirely behind the mountains before climbing to the top of a ridge to watch the light colored sky above the trees. Against a golden backdrop of the darkening sky we could easily see the trail of wood smoke from a campfire not half a mile away from us, just a short distance inside the tree line. Leading our horses, Frank and I closed the distance to a quarter mile. I was now wearing the moccasins I kept in my saddlebags along with the second colt I normally wrapped in the moccasins. Frank would stay with the horses as I crept close enough to their camp to discover how many there were and what they were planning. At the first sign of trouble Frank would gallop in leading my horse and we'd ride away to the north. I faded into the darkness with neither sound nor quick movement, creeping slowly toward the treachery surrounding their fire.

Circling carefully I was able to locate and avoid their horses. Just twenty yards from the camp fire I was able to hear nearly everything being said. Unafraid of being heard in the safety of their seclusion, they spoke freely and sometimes much too loudly. There were nine men in the camp, all of them bad news to have in the area. Not connected with any groups in the territory, they spoke of raiding our ranch the next day as they had done other ranches across the frontier when running short on money. They didn't like us being so close to Lincoln, but being north of the Capitans we were off the beaten path and not likely to have many visitors. The same reason we liked the ranch location was also cause for them to be attracted to us. In addition to the two men we followed there were seven

others, two who had been manning the morning shift at
their lookout and one who seemed to be the ramrod.
Some names were used, but none that sounded familiar
to me. Retreating back to Frank, I was able to remain
unnoticed. We led the horses slowly away to the west,
giving the outlaw camp a wide berth. Once south of
their camp and nearing the open desert we mounted.
Time was important now for the men would attack in
the morning. Since the moon was up we could see well
and trusting the horses to see better than us, we
alternated from a canter to a lope, circling our own
ranch and coming in from Aragon Creek, a direction
the raiders would not likely use. We preferred they not
see our sign when approaching the next day. Plans
must be made for the defense of our home and Frank
and I were the only ones having knowledge of the
impending attack.

We hit the ranch yard on the run, slowing as Bill and
Hank came out onto the porch rifles in hand. I called
for them to meet us in the barn, just the two of them.
Helping us with horses and tack, our brothers listened
seriously and we worked up a plan before joining the
others in the main house. They'd all been together
awaiting our return and with us galloping in at night,
everyone knew something was wrong.

Once in the house we met serious looks from the
rest of the family. Knowing were it not life threatening
we would neither have returned late nor run our horses
at night, they were anxious to hear our explanation.
The murderers had seen Frank and I ride toward
Lincoln this morning and figured us out of the picture.
We could use that to our advantage. Their plan was to
secretly take up positions in the barn once the men
finished their early chores and everyone was in the main

house for breakfast. Waiting for the men to return to their chores after breakfast, they would surprise and kill us one at a time if possible until the odds were more favorable. Then they would have their way about the ranch with the women and property until ready to leave later in the morning.

Our plan was a simple one, for those are usually the best and easiest to carry out. We gathered every gun we had between us and readied them for the next day's work. Since they figured Frank and I to be gone already we slept in the barn, taking turns standing watch. Guarding Maryellen's house would serve no purpose for the moment other than splitting us up, the raiders would figure it empty and pay it no mind. They planned on putting all their eggs in one basket and that was the barn. There they could surprise whichever men came out there for tools and chores after breakfast, thinning the opposition without the others hearing.

Concealed in the barn we'd be better able to protect our family from the initial attack and turn the tables on our attackers. That's when everyone in the house would join in the "festivities". To avoid a fight would be best, but that would not be allowed by this group. If Frank and I had attacked them in their camp we likely would have come out of it the worse for wear. Our only choice was to fort up and wait for them to come to us. It was a long night, but by morning everyone was rested enough for what lay ahead. My nephews, Matt and Luke, were young, but brought up right. They were as prepared for this as anyone could be. Good hunters they were handy with rifles and competent with their pistols. They would be dealt a full hand in the deadly game we are being forced to play.

CHAPTER ELEVEN

Frank nudged me awake before first light to be safe. We had taken hour long shifts through the night, sleeping lightly and spelling each other whenever we awoke from a nap. Just before sunup, Matt and Luke came out to the barn as usual for chores. This time they wore their converted colts hidden beneath their coats. Going about chores as they normally would, the boys worked their way to the barn. First Bill, then Howell came out and gathered up a couple of horses, saddling them in preparation for a short ride. They also helped to hide Frank and I in the north end of the loft, away from the house. We'd piled hay up to give us a little more concealment from the rest of the barn and spread slickers on top to stop burning embers of powder from catching the hay afire as we shot over top of it. Once the boys were almost finished, Maryellen came from her house carrying a pot of hot water to the main house and calling the men to breakfast. Steam from the pot painted a scene for the outlaws of her carrying hot food for breakfast. Unknown to the outlaws was the fact that having kept a watchful eye Maryellen had not taken the time to cook. The morning's meal had been prepared in the main house and the heavy steaming pot was simply part of a show intended to keep them unaware of our plans.

The morning sun was fully above the horizon when Bill and Howell walked into the main house followed by Luke and Matt who had tied a pair of saddled horses to the hitch rail near the steps. Several pair of eyes from inside the house would be watching all points of the compass for our unwanted company, in case their plan of attack had been altered during the night.

Frank and I lay still on the blankets we'd spread over the wooden floor of the loft. We both wore moccasins for quietness as we didn't want to make noise scuffing the planks when standing to carry out our counter ambush. Waiting without movement, we listened intently and watched each other's face for alarm. It didn't take long for the raiders to appear.

The first sign of our intruders came from our horses as they moved to the far end of the corral, one of them snorting, all of them staring intently to the northeast. The outlaws came into the barn from the corral, having approached on foot to conceal their movement by keeping the barn between themselves and the main house. They must have left their horses hidden in the draw about four hundred yards out. The first ones into the barn walked from one end to the other, making sure no one was there. Overconfident they never checked the loft. Once all nine of them were in the barn they began talking low, comparing notes and making sure none had seen anything out of the ordinary. The only thing different from the day before were the two saddled horses tied at the house. That delighted the outlaws who now thought our defenses would be down to only three men once the riders left.

Before long the front door to the main house came open. Luke and Hank stepped onto the porch carrying saddlebags and carbines, looking as if they had a good day's ride ahead of them. Bill and Matt followed, staying on the porch talking as the two riders lashed their gear to the saddles and mounted up. Matt spoke loudly, chiding Luke and Hank that he'd go and sit by the fire with another plate of eggs before taking up the day's work. As Luke and Hank finished talking with Bill they circled their horses a few times near the house before riding south as if toward Lincoln. Frank and I quietly adjusted our positions so we could see the marauders and could also come to our feet quickly when the time was right. We were not heard over the hoof beats of the circling horses, which had been part of our plan. Now we could plainly see the nine outlaws lined up across the opposite end of the barn watching the house through the only window on that wall, and cracks on either side of the doors.

After leaving the ranch yard Luke and Hank stepped up their pace to a trot, then angling behind the main house toward Aragon Creek they sped up to a canter. Luke must be sneaking back to the house now, since Hank was not to canter until Luke had hopped off his horse. Luke would use the house to conceal his return to the other side of his home from the bandits, much as they had used the barn to conceal their own approach. Hank would circle around to the east using the creek bank for cover, sealing the only direction of escape should any of the gang manage to get away from us. Moments later, Matt came out of the main house and walked from the porch, heading for the barn. Just then, Maryellen came onto the porch and called to Matt, asking him to bring the pot she was carrying back to her house before doing his chores. Matt, feigning reluctance, dutifully turned around to take the pot from his aunt and then walked to the other house.

Three of the waiting men in the barn were positioned near the door, planning to grab Matt as he came in. The others remained spread out along the far wall, their backs and sides facing us. There was no questioning their intent, nor any doubting what we must do.

Frank and I had coach guns to our shoulders as we straightened up just enough to clear the slicker covered hay. In unison we each fired two rounds of buckshot into the waiting men, breaking their ambush with our own. Though in line with the house, shooting downward our bullets would never escape the barn and posed no threat to anyone but the outlaws. My fire was concentrated on the three men waiting for Matt and I saw two of them fall. Frank's first shot took the man at the other end of the wall full in the back as he sat in ambush watching the house. His second shot hit a shelf above the group, showering them with tools and buckets distracting them as we moved to make our escape from the barn. We had the loft door unlatched already and after firing, instantly dropped our shotguns on the blankets and leapt from the loft to the ground outside. Instantly we ran for the north side of Maryellen's house. Matt was firing his carbine furiously from the porch window, covering our movement with fire directed into the partly open barn door and the gunmen facing him. Once behind the house Frank and I slid open an unlocked window and reaching in grabbed our rifles from where we'd placed them inside. Then taking up positions at opposite corners of the house behind the log abutments I'd built for such an occasion, we enjoyed a superior position. With us spread out at Maryellen's house and with those firing from the main house, we had a wide field of fire into the barn. It would be difficult for any surviving outlaws to escape unseen. Matt had two rifles and had emptied half of the first one, a Henry, covering our run. Figuring we'd had enough time for our move, he stopped firing for a time.

Frank and I both called out that we were unhurt and in position. Matt replied that he'd hit one of the outlaws who came partly outside of the barn tracking our run with a winchester. We could see him sprawled on the ground in the barn's doorway, breathing his last. Matt had likely saved at least one of us from the outlaw's rifle. Luke, who was inside the main house called that Bill had shot one who died trying to flank their position on the far side of the main house. Right about then we heard two quick shots from the porch window at the main house and heard another outlaw fall in the barn amidst the sound of cussing by the rest. Luke had spotted him preparing to shoot through the barn window and been quicker on the trigger. That left three of them still in the barn. We'd been very fortunate so far. It seems our surprise had been complete and we had the remaining bandits trapped with our superior positions and also badly outnumbered.

Frank and I had the north and west sides of the barn covered, Matt had the door. With Luke covering the south barn window facing the house and Bill watching the southeast corner of the barn, Howell emerged from the house carefully and took up a position behind the water trough in front of the porch. I called to the men in the barn and after a short pause got a curt answer. After ordering them to come out one at a time and unarmed we could hear some hurried movement from the barn. Then the first of the remaining bushwackers emerged from the barn door.

Howell called for him to slowly walk toward the water trough Howell was using for cover. The man complied, hands in the air. As he made a wide turn around the barn door, another of the men peaked around the door trying to get a shot at Howell with his pistol. Neither Matt nor Frank could see him because the first man blocked their view. Howell spotted the pistol's barrel coming around the door and levered three quick shots through the barn door itself. The pistol fell to the ground outside the doorway, still in the hand of the man who would have used it to kill Howell.

Now caught absolutely in the open, the man who had been ordered from the barn again started walking slowly toward Howell. He was a tall man, Howell's size and thickly built. But follow orders he did, at least for the time being. As the killer neared the water trough, Howell stood with rifle in hand, moving sideways so the prisoner was directly between him and the barn. This offered Howell some cover from the one remaining outlaw still in the barn. On command, the prisoner turned around to face the barn and Howell moved in, placing the muzzle of his rifle against the man's spine. There was a pistol tucked into the rougue's trousers in the small of his back and as Howell reached for it the man spun quickly, his elbow knocking the rifle barrel from his back. Howell triggered a shot but the muzzle was no longer on it's mark and the bullet flew off to the north somewhere. Howell was now in a wrestling match for his own rifle and the man's pistol as well. With all the quick movement none of us dared a shot.

Guns had flung off to the side, and the two big men grappled and struck each other in a fight for their lives. Before long Howell managed a good hold on the man, flung him to the side and reached for his own belted pistol. During the fight Howell's holster had slipped to the middle of his back and he was having trouble getting a quick hold of it. The outlaw reached for his own pistol as it lay in the dirt. Maryellen lept from the doorway of the main house onto the porch with a coachgun to her shoulder. She fired on the move as the outlaw tried to turn his gun toward Howell. Catching a full load of buckshot between the shoulder blades as he turned, the man twisted into the dirt as if a tree had fallen on him. Maryellen and Howell looked at each other for a brief moment before he grabbed his rifle and dove behind the water trough again. Maryellen calmly stepped back inside the house, having risked being shot from the barn in order to gain position for a shot none of the rest of us could have chanced from our positions. Her man was worth the risk.

Again I called to the barn, this time being answered by a voice I recognized from their campfire as the gang's leader. He was now also it's last living member. We could feel the reluctance in his voice as he agreed to come out. Wounded and limping as he walked from the barn holding a bloody left thigh he appeared beaten. Being the closest to him I stepped from the cover of my log abutment. With my rifle leveled at him we moved toward each other. Coming closer I noticed he still had a pistol in his waistband, almost hidden by the arm clutching his wounded leg. Figuring he thought the pistol hidden from all others I stopped him when we were about fifteen feet apart but still covered him with my Winchester. Telling him I could see the pistol I told him to carefully and slowly take it from his trousers and drop it in the dirt. Steely eyes and calm resolve betrayed his final attempt to fight as he slowly pulled the pistol and positioned it backwards in his right hand. With my rifle still pointed at him he extended the pistol to me butt first.

There would be no more harm done to him if he'd do as he was told. Having been in this situation before and confident of my own abilities, I decided to give him one last chance although it meant I would be risking myself at the same time. Recognizing his preparation for a "Road Agent Spin" and having checked my pistol before moving up, I released my right hand grip on the rifle and lowered the weapon to my left side. My right hand hovered near my pistol as the man's lips showed a slight grin. Watching his hand, I started slowly to move closer. As fingers opened to spin his pistol, I drew my own and fired just as his pistol completed it's spin. His thumb was beginning to contact the hammer but he still needed to draw it back. My bullet struck him just left of center in his chest and he straightened up still holding his un-cocked pistol. My second bullet hit right of center and his pistol dropped from his grasp. A surprised look coming across his face, he slowly toppled backwards into the dirt.

After cautiously checking the barn and yard to make sure no bandits remained a threat, Bill called for Sarah to ring the dinner bell. That was the arranged clear signal for Hank to come in from his position. Once in the creek, he circled around to the east and had located the outlaw's hidden horses. If any of them escaped our trap and made it to the horses, Hank would capture them if they allowed or send them to the next world if they made the wrong choice. It was a risky plan and placed Hank in a bad spot if we had failed to keep the bandits at the home site. But the fight had gone our way and Hank soon rode into the ranch yard with nine saddled horses strung out behind him.

We tied their horses alongside the corral and set about the chore of gathering the dead. We had taken stock of our own injuries and the most serious was some large slivers Matt had sticking in his arm. He'd received them when a bullet from the barn struck the door frame he was behind while covering Frank and I as we made our run to Maryellen's house. The good Lord had surely blessed us this fine day.

CHAPTER TWELVE

Matt was not injured seriously but still needed attention. Sarah dutifully took care of her youngest son's wound and had him patched up in no time. Luke, Howell, Hank and Frank were all detailed to gather the bodies and lay them in the cool shade of the barn floor for the time being. Bill and I collected the bandits' guns as we discussed our situation.

Only wanting to live our lives quietly, we were concerned about attracting attention while bringing so many bodies into Lincoln. As far as we could see though, there was no way around the need to do just that. Confidant that these men had nothing to do with either side of the trouble brewing in Lincoln County, it was agreed we would carry the men into Lincoln after eating a healthy brunch. Howell and Frank would stay at the ranch while the rest of the men rode to town. Bill needed to go because he is well respected and known as a good citizen not a trouble maker. Matt and Luke needed to go as this was their first brush with gunplay and they needed to see it through. They'd had a hand in defending the ranch and wanted dearly to help carry their attackers to town. Known as a lawman and already having an understanding with the marshal it was imperative that I lead our crew. It would be up to me to speak for us when we rode into town. Neither of the twins had been into town since coming to our ranch and after covering the outlaws' escape route that morning, Hank would also ride into Lincoln.

All the guns the outlaws had carried were top of the line and well taken care of. Luke, Matt and Bill each picked out new peacemakers from the pile and a new rifle as well. The boys' Spencer carbines, Bill's Henry and their Colt conversions would now rest in a cabinet at the ranch, for their new trophies were better weapons. We had found no identifying papers in their packs, so except for the weapons and ammunition carried by the gang we would bring all their belongings into town along with the bodies. After the boys made their picks we brought the rest of the guns inside. Howell and Frank would clean them while we were away. Extra guns for the ranch might come in handy someday so we held them all back when going into Lincoln. We hoisted the bodies across their saddled horses and tied them in place before going to the house for that well earned meal.

The ride into town took the rest of the day and we must have been a sight riding into Lincoln from the west with the sun low and at our backs. Riding at a slow walk, we were five riders leading nine horses with a body strapped across each of them. As we neared town, people in the street stared for a moment before scattering to tell everyone. By the time we pulled up near the marshal's office we had gathered quite a crowd. Everyone wanted to know who the dead men were and what had happened. They were trying to get a look at the dead faces as we walked up the street but nobody recognized any of them. Luke and Matt, unsure of what to do sat their horses as Bill, Hank and I dismounted to meet Sheriff Brady who had been standing in his doorway waiting on us for the last thirty yards of our approach.

After looking at the five of us he nodded toward Hank and asked me

"Who's this?"

"Name's Hank, he's an old friend and was a deputy of mine back in Arizona. He and his brother have been staying at the ranch with us a while."

Hank stepped up and extended a hand to the sheriff and Brady took it politely, sizing up Hank before moving toward the nearest corpse.

"How'd all this come to be?" He asked no one in particular as he moved the head for a look at it's cold face.

My brother started explaining and I filled in some of the story myself. The townsfolk listened in silence as we explained how the gang had been discovered and there had been no time to seek help. Everyone knew all too well that we had done what was necessary to defend our home and were lucky it had turned out well for us. It could easily have gone the other way as it has many times on the frontier.

Some time during the commotion, Amanda walked up and heard most of the story. When we finished explaining she walked over and took my arm. Then Sheriff Brady told us to wait a moment as he stepped into his office for a few seconds. He returned with a look-out flyer in his hand for an unidentified gang of marauders who had been raiding ranches in Arizona, stealing and killing all that got in their way.

Brady handed the flyer to Bill, looked at each of us and said:

"It looks like you boys have some reward money coming, these fellas are wanted pretty bad. There's a $5,000 reward offered for them, dead or alive."

Bill finished reading the flyer and passed it to me. We each read it before passing it on to the next, looking at each other with nods and slight smiles. It was easier to see Luke's and Matt's excitement than it was the rest of us, but that was understandable. The boys had been through a lot today and now were going to have more money than they'd ever seen before as their reward for a job well done.

Next I spoke to Sheriff Brady. "We kept their guns and ammunition but left all other belongings unmolested in their saddle bags and bedrolls."

"That sounds fair enough." He answered. "Their outfits will more than pay for burials and the rest will go into the town fund. I'll have them buried and wire for the reward money. Should have an answer on the money in a couple of days."

"Well Sheriff," I spoke up, "I think we could all use a nice meal and some rest so you can find us at the Wortley. Thanks for understanding."

We handed over the lead ropes to Brady and his people before heading for the hotel's livery. Walking with Amanda, I led my horse as the others mounted and rode up the street together, talking among themselves. So many things were going through my mind as we began our short trek to the hotel. Not liking to beat around the bush I figured to just go ahead and speak up.

"Amanda," I began, "A few days ago I decided the next time I came into town I would ask you about something. I just didn't know the reason I'd next be in town would be to settle up with the marshal after another fight."

"Well you didn't start this trouble, Slim, so you go right ahead and ask away." Amanda responded.

"I enjoy your company a great deal and would like you to come to the ranch for Thanksgiving dinner in a couple of weeks." There, I got most of it said and after a deep breath continued with Amanda listening carefully, "You can meet the rest of my family and see how we live. My sister has a house to herself and you could stay with her, Maryellen is her name. She can come into town with me and we'll bring you out to the ranch if you'd like to come."

Amanda had been holding my left hand in her right while we walked. She now reached across her body with her left hand and stopped walking.

Amanda placed her hand on my shoulder and softly said; "Bring your sister in, Slim. I'll be delighted to meet the rest of your family."

I nodded and walked a little straighter as we continued walking quietly up the street until reaching the Wortley's gate. There we parted with smiles and I stood by outside the gate with my horse until Amanda was again inside the restaurant to continue her work. I walked on to the livery and took care of my horse before joining my compadres in the hotel where we all cleaned up before supper.

We had two hotel rooms between the five of us so we just sort of mingled between the rooms as we tidied up and brushed the dust from our clothing. When we walked into the restaurant we were ushered right away to a table big enough for our whole crew to sit without crowding each other. The dining room was about three fourths of the way full and most of the eyes in the room were on us by the time we reached our table and sat down. Most of the people were smiling at us and a few of the men told us they were happy we had made out alright in our scrape with the outlaws. Watching Luke and Matt, excited as they were but at the same time embarrassed by the attention, was a source of amusement for the rest of us. You just don't know how a man will react after killing another man, even when he must. I was relieved the boys were fine and not bothered by the day's events.

In just a short time, Amanda was at our table. There was a new gleam in her eye and comfort in her manner as we visited briefly. Bill and the boys knew her somewhat but I reintroduced them anyway. After meeting Hank, Amanda kidded with Luke and Matt a little bit before taking our orders. As hungry as we were we all just followed Bill's lead and ordered the same thing. Meat and potatoes with some greens makes a great meal! Amanda brought us all water and even a glass of cool milk for the boys. A nice basket of fresh baked bread and a slab of butter gave us something to start in on while we talked and waited for the main course.

Our whole crew was a bit on the tired side and once we started eating there wasn't much conversation. I guess right then we were more interested in the food than each other. The main course was topped off with a big piece of apple pie for each of us. We all agreed it was as delicious as any we'd ever had. The excitement of the day took it's toll on us and after finishing off the pie, it didn't take long for the boys to start getting tired. Everyone went back to the rooms except my brother and I. We headed for the barn to check the horses. Not that they needed checking but we just wanted to get away from the noise of all the people and let the day's activities sort of settle in.

After letting Bill know that Amanda had agreed to come to the ranch for Thanksgiving, he joked that we'd better get back home early so everyone would know things had worked out in town. We needed to return in time for Howell and the twins to get started for

Albuquerque and the wagons. If they didn't start within the next few days they might end up missing out on the holiday meal! Bill headed back to the rooms and I meandered over to the restaurant porch. There I took up my "post" in a chair, to wait for Amanda and a pleasant walk to her house. Town was fairly quiet and the only activity I could see was a young family finishing their dinner in the restaurant.

After the restaurant closed up for the night Amanda came onto the porch with Ralph, the owner. He told me how relieved he was that the fight at our ranch had turned out as it had. Continuing on, Ralph told me that he had been unsure what sort of man I was that first day we met. When he had tried to warn me about Sam and found out I knew Sam already, he thought I might just be another bad sort like Sam. He also explained how getting to know me better has convinced him I am a good and just man. I think Ralph was giving me a sort of "fatherly" talk since next he explained to me how he and his wife feel Amanda is really like part of their family and they have worried about her in this town where there is so much turmoil. He thanked me for walking Amanda home in the evenings when I'm in town and told me he'll be alright with the restaurant while Amanda visits our ranch. It felt awkward and I'm sure it was a difficult conversation for him to start, but it showed me the kind strength Ralph has when it comes to something or someone dear to him.

The walk to Amanda's was slow and quiet. We walked arm in arm and spoke very little. The "goodnight" we exchanged included a very soft and gentle kiss before Amanda disappeared inside. As usual I waited a short time after the lamp was lit, making sure

Amanda remained safe before making my way back to the hotel and a good night's sleep.

CHAPTER THIRTEEN

The next morning began before daylight as usual for me. Even though I had no plans for the day, years of waking before first light out of necessity conditions a man's body. That's one habit I don't mind having for it's a good one in this part of the country and has kept more than a few folks alive from time to time. But on this day there was no hurry. The sun peaked over the hills to the east of town as I was walking to the livery and our horses.

Visiting with the liveryman, I helped him feed the animals in his care and prepare for his day's work. He owns a blacksmith shop next to the hotel's livery and does a lot of business with hotel guests. Splitting the livery fees with the hotel earns him some extra cash and works out well for both businesses. While moving around the smithy I noticed he was set up with a bath, not a public one, but a nice private bath. Since I would be around town for a couple of days waiting for news on the reward, a bath would be nice. After making a deal to come back later for a bath I went back to the hotel, joining Bill and the others as they left for breakfast at the restaurant.

We were there early, before most of the regular crowd. The meal was a fine one and we took our time finishing it. Amanda visited as her work allowed. When we left, the five of us walked together up to Tunstall's store. This country is hard on clothes and over breakfast I told everyone I was going to buy a fresh pair of pants and a shirt before taking a bath. They all thought being clean while we stayed in town was a good idea and decided to follow my lead. Not wanting to waste a trip to town we also left a list of supplies with the clerk at Tunstall's. A list of supplies thatwould be useful at the ranch to help us last a couple of weeks until the next trip to town before Thanksgiving. We'd pick up the order whenever it was time for us to leave again.

Still not in a hurry we took our time in the store. Matt and Luke wore hats that were getting a little ragged and Tunstall had a good supply of Stetsons so I offered to buy the boys each a new one. With smiles on their faces the boys agreed they'd like the hats. Eventually we left the store carrying our clothes and headed for the bathhouse. I went to Bud's blacksmith shop for my bath.

By noontime we were all clean and those of us who needed it had a shave too. We all wore our new clothes, our old ones were being cleaned and folded. Back to the Wortley's restaurant for lunch, we were busy eating when Marshal Ollinger came looking for us with news of the reward money. Turns out the $5,000 listed on the flyer we'd seen was old news and another $3,000 had been added to it after an Arizona raid two weeks before. We were looking at $8,000 cash and Ollinger had me sign for a wire from the Phoenix Bank authorizing payment to me.

We discussed the money while finishing lunch and with Hank speaking for Frank we agreed that the twins not actually being part of the family should get an even one thousand dollars. The rest of us, each member of the family both men and women, would each get five hundred dollars put into an account for them. Howell being almost an official family member, but also starting a business, should get a thousand dollars too. That left two thousand to put in the ranch account and save for a rainy day. The ranch is making out alright and doesn't need anything at the moment so we'll just save the rest of the money for when we do.

After finishing lunch, Hank and the two boys packed up their belongings before heading back to the ranch. Bill and I will follow in the morning after finishing up arrangements with the money this afternoon.

Both of the boys, Luke and Matt, really looked slick in their new duds. Just like a healthy head of beef with no ribs showin' and a slick coat of fur. Headed for the ranch, Hank, Luke and Matt rode out of town at a slow lope. Matt and Luke sitting tall, enjoying the feel of being clean, everyone they saw waving a greeting as they passed by. Men now, having survived a righteous battle victoriously, they rode side by side with their friendly partner Hank, one of the most imposing figures they'd ever seen. Hank was wearing a smile too, because having been there before, he remembered how the boys felt. He knew these were good boys, with a new confidence in themselves, a confidence he shared.

After we watched the others disappear around a bend in the road, Bill and I turned back inside Tunstall's to tend our banking needs. Two thousand dollars went into an account for Hank and Frank, one thousand into Howell's business account and the balance after paying our bill went into the ranch's account. It was a family operation and we all knew the boys had money coming to them when they needed it. As far as my money was concerned, well, I was part of the ranch now too.

As we left the store, the clerk was finishing packing our supplies in sacks we could tie to our horses for the ride back to the ranch in the morning. Bill and I walked slowly toward the hotel, stopping near the torreon to laugh at some memories from our childhood. We were in no particular hurry as we had the rest of the afternoon to relax and enjoy the companionship only two brothers could share. Turning in at the Worley, Bill and I sat in a pair of large comfortable wooden chairs made by a local craftsman. They were wide enough to allow our gunbelts ample room and tall enough to lean our heads back. We removed our hats and truly relaxed in these chairs. Spending the rest of the afternoon quietly, our conversations alternated between planning for the future, remembering the past and falling silent while we sat and looked over the quiet town. Amanda joined us from time to time, bringing lemonade to sweeten away the bitter taste of the cigars Bill and I had purchased at Tunstall's. We all agreed this was a nice town and hoped the building tensions within it had been quieted by the raid at our ranch.

During one of the lulls in our conversation I

realized how relaxed I was becoming after the raid. It was a good, comfortable feeling I hadn't experienced in many years. Like a huge weight had been lifted from my shoulders. When Bill first sent for me I knew the kind of trouble he was expecting, and that he was counting on me to help them survive. We had survived and that responsibility had been met. But I'd been through fights like this before and there was more to my feelings than just that. I suppose that relief coupled with the increasing likelihood that Amanda and I were building something is what had me feeling so relaxed.

Lincoln County would be quiet for a time after a raid like this, but only for a time. The trouble brewing under the surface was deep and still simmering. The fight my brother was wary of when he sent for me had not yet happened although it surely lay on the trail before us. My family's happiness and the chance of a future with Amanda could all be gone in the flash of a muzzle if I stayed too relaxed for too long. Relaxed I would be and a happy, fruitful life is what I would pursue. But complacency kills, so I will always be watchful for trouble.

James Hollmann